Michelle

SPRINGSONG ✿ BOOKS

Kara
Lisa
Michelle

SPRINGSONG ❧ BOOKS

Michelle

Eva Gibson

BETHANY HOUSE PUBLISHERS
MINNEAPOLIS, MINNESOTA 55438

Michelle
Eva Gibson

Library of Congress Catalog Card Number 83-72409

ISBN 1-55661-447-0

Published by Bethany House Publishers
A Ministry of Bethany Fellowship, Inc.
11300 Hampshire Avenue South
Minneapolis, Minnesota 55438

Printed in the United States of America

For my granddaughters,

Jeni Leigh

and

Kyndi Joy

EVA GIBSON loves writing fiction, especially mysteries for teens. She is the author of several studies and ten books. Her latest book for teen girls is *Listening to My Heart*, a handbook on journaling (Bethany House, 1990).

Eva lives in Wilsonville, Oregon, her home state, with her husband Bud. They have six grown children and eight grandchildren. Her hobbies are backpacking, pressing flowers, and reading. She also enjoys teaching Bible studies in her home church and speaking at various women's retreats and workshops.

Contents

1

On the Banks of
Eagle Creek

*M*icky might have been a sculpture carved atop the gray boulder. Her silky hair lay dark against the April sky, her deep green sweatshirt distinct from, yet blending with, the barely budded alders.

Beyond her still frame, the creek flashed and roared and rippled and spit a fine white spray. Then it changed—swirling, glinting—the quieter pools along the edges reflecting sky and trees, hinting at life far below.

"You dear, majestic, wild stream," Micky murmured. "You're so alive—so vibrant. I'd like to get to know you . . . find out why they call you Eagle Creek."

She hunched forward on the sun-drenched rock; a slight girl, with dark hair framing a small, heart-shaped face, her dark eyes dreamy, Micky's thoughts were caught up in the music of the stream. She lowered her hand into the icy water.

He spoke from behind her. "Seen any fish?"

Micky whirled around, her hands spraying cold drops onto her jeans. Her eyes flashed with momentary fear, reflecting something of the creek's mysterious depths.

But it was only a smiling young man who stood behind her, a fishing pole in one hand, a tackle box in the other. He was encased to the waist in heavy rubber waders, making Micky wonder how he'd crept up so softly.

But it was his hair that caught her attention and kept her eyes riveted on him. It was reddish brown and curlier than any hair she had ever seen.

"Seen any fish?" he repeated.

"No," Micky mumbled, "not that I know of."

In one quick jump he cleared the water between the bank and Micky's broad boulder. He looked at her with open curiosity and gestured toward the pink house behind them. "Friends of the Middletons?" he asked.

"Not exactly," she said. "I'm—I'm living there—"

"Really?" Surprise edged his voice. "Then you must be in our school."

Micky squirmed uncomfortably. "I'm not in school," she said.

The young man shook his head. "You could have fooled me."

"I'm only sixteen," Micky countered. "I haven't graduated—"

There was another long, thoughtful look from the young man. But he didn't ask any more questions. Instead, he smiled.

"I'm Joel Brentwood. Kent lets me come and fish here anytime I want to, but I live in Estacada."

Micky relaxed visibly. "That last little town you go through before you get here?"

He nodded. "I'll be a senior in high school next year. I come up here as often as I can to fish. There's just something about this creek—" He broke off suddenly. "Do you fish?"

"No."

Enthusiasm lifted his chin. Micky looked at him intently. *His eyes are that unusual, strange color between gray and green,* she thought. *Like mother's were . . .*

Joel laughed out loud in obvious delight. "I'll teach you—whatever your name is."

Micky smiled. "It's Micky . . . Michelle Ann Strand. I'm a ward of the court now," she volunteered. "Kent and Loretta Middleton are my new foster parents. I've never lived in the country before. It's always been the big city—"

"Must be really different for you here. . . ." He gestured toward the rushing water. "Well, how about it? Want me to show you how to fish?"

Micky nodded. "Sure."

Joel put his tackle box beside her. "May I?"

Micky peered inside. There were hooks, spinners, plugs, and dainty flies of every description. She gently touched a rainbow-hued one.

Joel reached for a hook, ignoring the alluring flies. He uncapped a jar of pink salmon egg clusters. "Right now those biggies out there are taking eggs," he explained, nodding toward the creek. "Yesterday I got three on. Brought one home, too."

He waded out into the water, his waist-high boots changing the pattern of the rushing creek. *He's tall,* she thought, *his curly head would even be above Kent's.*

Joel flicked his wrist, and his line drifted into the middle of the creek. He looked back at Micky.

"Go up to the house," he suggested, "and ask Loretta for a pair of these." He patted his boots. "They've got lots of poles, too. Kent would be awfully glad to see you fishing." He nodded toward the house. "They all fish—even Loretta."

A deep excitement stirred inside Micky. Oh, to be out there in the middle of that wonderful rushing creek . . .

She jumped to her feet, leaped across the small rocks, and ran up the bank. She scurried to the basement entrance, pausing only long enough to take a deep breath of the heavenly white blossoms foaming over the giant cherry tree planted close to the house. Then she was inside, up the stairs, and into the kitchen. "Loretta, could I learn to fish?"

Loretta turned, a slow smile widening her mouth. "Why, Micky. That would be fine." She wiped her hands on a paper towel. She was a pleasant, attractive woman, with soft dark hair pulled back and held with a narrow black band.

"We've got lots of extra equipment downstairs. I'll set you up." She led the way into the daylight basement room that served as a family room. Her eager voice trailed behind. "We're a fishing family, you know. Living on the creek like this, it's sort of expected, I suppose."

She opened a door at the bottom of the stairs. Micky peered past her. An assortment of boots tumbled on the floor, poles lurked in corners, various jackets hung from hooks, as did a pair of long boots dangling on suspenders.

"You'll need these, now," Loretta explained, handing the boots to Micky. "The rain we've had this spring has raised the creek." A frown creased Loretta's face as she reached for a pole. "Someone will need to show you—" she said cautiously.

"It's all right," Micky interrupted. "There's a Joel

somebody down on the rock. He has salmon eggs and everything. He said he'd show me how to fish!"

"Oh—yes, Joel. That's great. Run along and have fun." She started up the stairs.

The big boots flopped awkwardly across Micky's arm and bumped against her knees as she hurried down the slope. But the pole in her hand felt smooth and good, almost as though it belonged there.

She leaned it against the big rock and clambered up. "I got a strike!" Joel called. "But he's gone. Put your boots on."

Micky watched him as he turned and waded toward her. Even in the water his movements were free and easy, held in by a quiet controlled vitality. He smiled at her and she blushed. Awkwardly she pulled on the tall boots.

"They're too big!" she laughed, holding the floppy sides.

Joel agreed. "It won't matter though," he said. "They'll keep you dry."

Carefully he selected an egg cluster and baited her hook. Together they waded into the icy stream, the water pushing against their legs, filling Micky with a strange excitement. But the pole that had felt so graceful on the way to the creek suddenly seemed like an over-sized pencil, stiff and awkward.

"I'll help," Joel volunteered. Gently he rearranged her hands around the rod. Micky threw her shoulders back and made a perfect cast. It drifted over the ripples and sank into a shady pool.

"All right!" Joel exclaimed. "There's fish there, too. I saw them, down deep—big steel gray—" He waded away from her downstream. "Just watch . . ."

He cast again—a long, graceful arc—and the line

shone silver. Micky's pole quivered, her line suddenly taut. She hung tight while Joel came back and handed her his rod.

"It's one of the hazards," he explained as he set her line free from a submerged log.

Micky was undaunted. She cast again, but this time her hook caught in the alders over her head.

Somehow she was caught off-balance and thrown to her knees. The creek immediately filled her huge boots and pulled her downward—down—down—down—until it was over her head.

Dimly she heard Joel shout as she went under, "Don't panic!"

But she did. The icy water rushing over her head, the weight of the boots welding her beneath the gushing stream. Cold terror froze her thoughts. She released the pole and grasped blindly for something to hold onto.

Then Joel's hands were on her shoulders, yanking her up into the blessed air. She gasped, clawing at his shirt.

Through a film of water she glimpsed fear on his face. Then she screwed her eyes shut and hung on. Together they stumbled to the shore.

"I'm so sorry—" she whispered. "I should have been more careful—"

Then they were beside a big rock. Micky let go of his shirt. She clung to the rock's sun-warmed edge.

"Get rid of those waders," he advised. Micky's icy fingers fumbled with the suspenders on her shoulders. She pushed off the heavy rubber from her waist and sat down abruptly, shivering. Joel got on his knees and began pulling off her boots, the water gushing from them and pooling around his legs.

Then, with his soft flannel shirt in his hand, he was

wiping her face. Micky looked at him through drenched lashes and tried to smile. Trembling, he took the shirt and rubbed her dripping hair.

There was an angry shout from the bank. "Joel!"

Micky and Joel turned abruptly.

It was Kent. He was a tall, lean, often angry man, and now he stood, his legs stiff and braced apart. "Don't you know better than to let her go out so deep? She could have drowned!"

Joel got to his feet and went toward Kent. But Kent paid no attention to him.

"Go inside, Micky!" he shouted. "We don't want a sick kid around here!" Abruptly, without another word, he wheeled away.

Micky stared after him in shock. "Kent's pole," she whispered in sudden consternation. "It's gone—" She shivered.

"Don't worry," Joel muttered. "I'll find it if I can. Just go in and get dried out." He gave her shoulder a gentle shove.

Her clammy sweatshirt clung to her body as she stumbled up the bank toward the house. Loretta met her at the door, a bathrobe and towel in her hand, worry clouding her gray eyes.

"He's awfully angry—" Micky faltered. She touched Joel's flannel shirt still draped around her dark mop. Great shivers ran through her body. Loretta reached for the edge of her sweatshirt and helped her wriggle out of it.

"Try not to be upset," she said.

"But why should he lash out like that at Joel?" she asked between chattering teeth.

Obvious pain etched lines into Loretta's face. "We've had a drowning here . . ." Her voice faded. She pushed the robe into Micky's hand. "Take off those soggy jeans and have a hot shower," she advised, nodding toward the bathroom adjoining the family room. "Come down when you're dry."

She turned abruptly and went up the stairs. Micky looked after her. Why had that haunted look suddenly masked Loretta's face? Why had Kent gotten so angry over a simple mishap? He'd been peaceable enough that first time—except . . .

When she first met Kent the kitchen was warm, scented with a simmering roast. He was sitting at the kitchen table, a newspaper spread before him. He'd smiled when Loretta put her arm around Micky and presented her to her husband.

"This is Kent," she had said, her gray eyes dancing. "He thinks all girls are special. Even shy ones with big, dark eyes like yours."

Kent had smiled. He started to reach for Micky's hand, then drew back. He scowled, turning abruptly to Loretta. "Why don't you show her to her room?"

Micky had felt shattered. *He doesn't like me*, she thought. *I wonder why. . . .*

Following Loretta through the living room, she'd comforted herself by thinking, *But Loretta does. She said so*.

Now Micky pushed her memories aside and undid the flannel shirt wrapped around her head. For a moment she buried her face in its damp softness.

As she did, another dark thought occurred to her. Had someone they loved been dragged beneath that cold, icy water? Loretta had said, "We've had a drowning here." Micky shivered and hurried into the bathroom.

2

"They Don't Want Me!"

"*I* don't like this room," Micky mumbled, "and it doesn't like me." She sat down on the edge of the pink ruffled bedspread and reached for her tennis shoes.

"It really doesn't fit this family," she continued, tying her laces. "And neither do I."

She pulled out a pair of blue jeans and a warm turtleneck sweater from the dresser. She put them on, her eyes examining the details of the room: The pink ruffled curtains matched the dressing table skirt and bedspread, complementing the deep rose carpet. There was a delicate ballerina lamp on a dainty flared doily atop the dresser. Even in the picture over the bed, white kittens with pink bows shouted, "Fragile, handle with care!"

How strange for an outdoor, country family to keep a room like this, she thought. "They should have done it in earthy colors to go with the rest of the house and the outdoors," she decided aloud. "Surely not deep rose carpet with pale pinks and white."

She combed her hair into some semblance of order and drifted into the living room. Now here was a room! Plain beige drapes were drawn back to reveal the greening leaves outside, the foaming, rushing stream, the great blossoming cherry tree.

Creamy wallpaper with light etchings of green ivy

covered the walls, and big stuffed chairs and scattered cushions carried an invitation to curl up and enjoy the gifts of the great outdoors. And that was just what Steve Middleton was doing.

Sprawled in a corner chair, surrounded by scattered comic books, his blue-gray eyes regarded Micky solemnly. He nodded toward the window. "I saw you out there."

Memories of those icy rushing waters brought goose bumps out on Micky's arms. She shivered.

"You almost drowned," Steve added.

Micky's chin jerked. "Not really. Joel pulled me out in an instant—and I can swim.

Steve shook his head. "It holds you down," he said.

Micky shrugged. "So? But I didn't drown, did I?" She plopped into a chair and regarded him curiously.

Since she'd arrived at the Middletons, she'd seen little of Steve. After school he slipped through the house like a shadow.

Even at meals he kept his chin down, his eyes averted. His conversation was limited to, "Pass the milk, please." "Thank you." "Excuse me."

But something sparkled in his eyes now. Micky smiled at him, gesturing at the scattered comics.

"Do you read a lot?"

He nodded, his thoughts quite obviously not on the books. "You sure got Dad upset."

Micky squirmed uncomfortably. "I don't understand that. I never meant to."

"He gets like that when he's scared," Steve observed knowingly. "He wasn't even thinking of you, not really."

"Not thinking of me? I was the one under the water!" Micky sputtered. "What do you mean?"

That hooded look covered his eyes again. He looked at his opened book and turned a page.

———

Dinner that evening was a solemn affair. Kent avoided meeting Micky's eyes, and Loretta had little to say. If it hadn't been for Steve, Micky was sure she wouldn't have been able to eat a bite. Somehow her afternoon episode seemed to have changed his attitude toward her.

His blue eyes caught her attention over the steaming stew and hot biscuits. "You look like you never fished before," he observed.

Micky shook her head.

"Did you like it?"

"I—I—Yes, I did, or at least I think I will after I've had more practice."

"The creek will close to anglers in a few days," he said, "but you can practice casting where the little trees are planted. That's what I did."

An uncomfortable silence followed. Micky determinedly buttered her biscuit and took a bite. Steve looked up, caught her eye again, and grinned encouragingly.

Micky looked from Kent to Loretta, but both were concentrating on their food, Kent dishing up another bowl of stew, and Loretta poking at a potato, a slight frown creasing her forehead.

Afterward, Micky helped Loretta with the dishes, then went to her room. But its fragile, pristine beauty repelled her. She wanted to be outside, to absorb all the warmth she could from what remained of the frail spring sunshine.

But as she stepped out of the frilly pink room, her

eye caught sight of a door to her left. It was slightly re-
cessed and she hadn't noticed it before. Curiously, she
opened it and saw steep narrow stairs yawning upward
before her. She fumbled for the light switch, but nothing happened when she turned it on.

Funny, she thought. *I hadn't thought about there being another floor in the house.* There was a door at the top
of the stairs. She could see its vague outline in the faint
light from the hall.

She went up slowly, her footsteps cautious on the
uncarpeted treads. She tried the door, but it was locked.

Why would anyone keep an inside door locked? Micky
wondered. She tried it again, but it firmly resisted her
efforts.

Micky ran down the stairs, through the living room,
and out the front door. Already the sun had disappeared
behind the trees, and the air was cooling.

She reached the edge of the lawn and turned. Sudden excitement throbbed through her. The upstairs
window at the back of the house was partially obscured
by the cherry tree branches, but it faced the creek.

What a view! What a retreat, with the creek rushing
and roaring beneath it, and the cherry tree, that great
white-blossomed giant right outside the window!

She ran her fingers through her dark hair, wondering if Loretta would let her unlock and explore the
room. Memories of Loretta's and Kent's preoccupation
at dinner made her doubtful.

Micky raced across the grass. High above her
stretched the great branches of the cherry tree. She
grabbed one of the lower branches and vaulted into the
crotch of the tree.

She looked up. The top curled over her like a white
canopy. She took a deep breath and exulted in the blos-

soms' subtle sweetness. High above her head the upstairs window seemed to beckon.

"I'm coming, I'm coming," she whispered. She clasped the tree trunk with one hand and, with the other, reached for a limb above her head.

Branch by branch she mounted higher in the tree. She paused and looked down. Everything looked different: the top of the barely greening snowball bush, the rosy pink of the flowering quince, and tiny gold dandelions studding the lawn. Across the yard the birch swirled tender new leaves, announcing its own spring debut.

Micky climbed higher. When she was even with the window, she inched forward on the limb. The bark pushed against her stomach and she lay cat-like, peering through the glass.

There was a bed inside with a bright-colored Indian blanket, a round multi-colored rag rug on the floor, and a plain maple chest of drawers. "Ooh," she murmured, "it looks so cozy. I wonder . . ."

"Micky!" Loretta called. "Micky!"

Micky opened her mouth to answer, then shut it determinedly. Climbing fruit trees had been firmly forbidden by more than one foster parent. A picture of Kent's dark anger made her shiver.

Carefully, she backed along the branch until she reached the comparative safety of the inner branches, which were shaped like a pair of bird wings. She smiled and eased into them, her back comfortable against the warm bark.

For a moment she dreamed of the upstairs room—the open window facing the tree, the creek roaring its music day and night. Perhaps she could have friends there, too. She wasn't sure what they'd look like, but she could see their hazy outlines—one in the middle of the bright Indian blanket, the other cross-legged on the rug. A sweet sadness rose in her throat.

"A place of my own," she murmured, "a place of my very own."

She'd been saying that for as long as she could remember.

Her earliest memory transported her to a faded yellow house with a big porch. Her father honked the horn and they started off with a jerk, boxes and baggage rattling. Tucked in the back of a station wagon with her two brothers, she turned and watched the only home she'd ever known fade away.

After that came a jumbled succession of curtainless kitchens, battered linoleum, and Kevin's crib shoved in any handy corner.

"A place of my own." She said it or thought it every time she stepped into a new house. It had been on the tip of her tongue when she'd arrived at the Middletons four days ago. She was saying it again now—

She looked down. The surging water seemed to beckon. She smiled, remembering Joel. There had been something about his eyes. They were like the stream— no, more gentle, kind. She wondered if she'd ever see him again.

A door below her closed. She looked back at the window to the room and muttered, "I shouldn't, but I'm going to."

Once again she inched along the limb. The window was so close. Tentatively she released her hold on the branch and touched the ledge. Then she cautiously slid forward, the branch still firm beneath her. Her hand met the window glass and she gave it a push. It opened easily, and Micky scrambled inside.

The room was all she had dreamed and more. It was L-shaped, and the half she hadn't seen through the glass boasted a desk and another window. Micky opened it and leaned far out. The stream's voice and the fresh scent of firs mingled their welcome. She caught her breath.

"I'm home! I'm home!" she exulted. She drew in her head and did a quick whirling dance in the middle of the room before collapsing on the rug.

She looked around. Knotty pine slanted across the sloping ceiling. The same paneling covered the walls. A closet door, slightly ajar, invited her scrutiny.

Micky jumped up and opened it wide. A jumble of empty jars, books, a baseball mitt, and an old stocking hat met her eyes. Curiously she moved them aside to see a fishing rod, a scrapbook, a small carving of a deer . . .

"Micky!" Loretta's voice wafted in through the open window.

Quickly, Micky pushed the things inside and shut the closet door. At the window she turned, "Goodbye, hideaway in the sky."

She descended hurriedly, first one branch, then another. And then . . .

"We wanted a younger child—one who was more, you know—more moldable—and more feminine . . ."

Micky froze, hardly daring to breathe. She leaned forward, pushing a perfumed branch to one side. She saw the narrow headband in Loretta's smooth dark hair and heard another voice murmur something unintelligible.

The heat rose in Micky's face. Swiftly, she grasped the branch at her feet with her hands and swung, monkey-fashion, onto the ground.

She ran for the basement door, then stopped. Loretta and her unseen friend would probably be upstairs, and there would be no way to avoid them unless, unless . . .

She turned and scuttled around the house, creeping behind the garage. Her window was open. It only took a moment to wriggle inside.

She stuffed a change of underwear, an extra shirt and jeans, and a comb into her brown duffel bag, then she was out the window and away.

The only road leading away from the house was steep and curved like a coiled snake. She left the road and headed for the brush, scrambling straight up the hillside. Her chest began to ache and her breath came in short little gasps before she slowed to a limping climb.

"They don't want me," she whispered. "Not Kent, not Steve, not even Loretta!"

The hurt slithered up and wrapped itself around her throat. She tried to concentrate instead on the soft, steep slope, spongy with fir needles. Then the road was before her again.

She hesitated briefly, then leaped the ditch. Once across, she leaned against the rough bark of a straight, tall fir and looked back.

A bird winged high over her head, flying in the direction of the stream—her stream, at least it had been for a few days. Through the trees she glimpsed the Middletons' pink house with the fish hatchery and its adjacent buildings stretched before it. The view made her think of the bottom of a great bowl, and she, high on its edge, looking down into it.

A sudden thought stabbed her. *I never got a chance to visit the hatchery.* And then, *I'll never see my hideaway in the sky again, either. Oh, if only it had been the place . . .*

She shivered. The warmth of the afternoon sun was gone. She turned, the hillside, thickly carpeted with ferns and wild strawberry plants, ascended before her. Dusky shadows lurked beneath the trees.

But Micky went forward. The branches caught her shoulder-length dark hair, moss clung to her sweater.

She stumbled again onto the graveled country road. It was already dusk and a lone star winked at her. A large bird swooped close to her head. Then an unidentified dark bulk loomed in front of her and brilliant headlights shone through the gloom, momentarily blinding her.

Micky's fingers tightened on her duffel bag. She swallowed miserably. Loretta got out of the car and walked to the other side, opening the door.

"Get in, Micky," Loretta said. "I've been waiting here for you."

A part of Micky wanted to whisper, "I'm sorry, Loretta," but the other part cried, "Why did you come after me? You don't really want me! Do you?"

Numbly she climbed into the car. "How did you know I was gone?" she asked.

"I wanted you to meet my friend, Lucille. When I couldn't find you, I went to your room. Your drawers were open—"

"Why—why did you come after me?" she whispered, struggling to keep her voice from breaking.

"Why do you think?" Loretta asked, slipping behind the wheel.

Micky peered through the darkness, trying to see Loretta's face. She opened her mouth, but no words came.

"I came because I care about you," Loretta said slowly.

"No you don't!" Micky cried. "I heard—"

"What is it you think you heard?"

"You said you had wanted someone younger! Someone more—more feminine—"

Loretta's arm suddenly slid around Micky's shoulders. "You didn't hear the rest, did you."

"I—I—"

"I told Lucille that was the child I had in my mind. But as soon as I saw you, I knew you were the one I wanted to take into my home—my heart."

"But—"

"I know. Try to understand, Micky. What people have in mind isn't necessarily what they really want. As soon as I saw your big dark eyes, that fly-away soft, dark hair, I knew—"

"But Kent—"

Loretta's arm tightened around her. "Kent has his own private torment to deal with. And I—Please, Micky, won't you give us a chance?"

Micky turned toward her in the darkness, a funny warm feeling rising inside her. Was it true? Did Loretta really care about her?

She did come after me, Micky reasoned. *If she didn't care, she wouldn't have, would she?* Micky leaned back in the seat, her thoughts a jumble of too many new feelings, new impressions.

Together they drove back down the curvy, winding road. Back to the stream—and—Micky drew in her breath sharply—Joel?

3

At the Fish Hatchery

*M*icky awoke the next morning to the smell of frying bacon. She licked her lips and bounced out of bed.

She stepped easily into her blue jeans while she debated whether to wear the plaid shirt or the dark blue pullover.

She decided on the blue pullover and pulled it on, critically examining her reflection in the mirror—tousled dark hair, almond-shaped eyes that looked too small for her heart-shaped face, lips needing a touch of color.

Then Kent's unexpected roar, "Breakfast! Come and get it!" galvanized her to action. She whisked the comb through her hair before another shout propelled her through the door.

Kent stood in front of the kitchen stove, legs braced apart, brandishing a spatula. He grinned at her, yesterday's animosity clearly gone.

"Sit down," he invited. "I'll dish up for you."

He thrust a plate in front of her, piled high with steaming scrambled eggs and crisp bacon. Steve slid into the chair opposite her and lifted his eyebrows, then gave her a long, slow wink.

An unexpected sense of belonging enfolded Micky. She grinned back at him.

27

"It's Saturday," Steve said. "Want to tour the fish hatchery with me?"

"Do they let you do that?" Micky asked, trying to conceal her excitement.

"Sure do." He took a big bite of the eggs on his plate. "A lot of the guys who work there are my friends now. I go over there a lot."

"It sounds interesting," Micky said tentatively. "Can we go inside the buildings?"

"They take people through all the time," Loretta said from the doorway.

She smiled at her husband and sat down beside Micky. Loretta looked fresh and young, dressed in a crisp red-striped blouse and dark slacks. "Where's my breakfast?" she asked teasingly.

"Adam and Eve on a raft and wreck'em!" Kent answered with the name of her favorite style of eggs. He plopped the eggs deftly onto a piece of toast and carried Loretta's plate to her with exaggerated flair.

Micky turned away as Kent bent to kiss his wife. Loretta didn't seem the least embarrassed.

"So, it's the fish hatchery for you, is it?" she asked Micky.

Steve stood up and mumbled, "Excuse me, meet you out front," and vanished out the door.

Kent scowled after him. "I wish he wouldn't do that eat-and-run business."

Loretta was unperturbed. "He'll grow up fast enough. Kids, do you know—"

Kent pushed back his chair and went for the door. "Steve!" he roared. Bits of his angry lecture drifted back through the open door: ". . . ungrateful, discourteous; you only think of yourself."

Loretta got up and began to clear the table. "Let me," Micky volunteered.

"No, thanks. Go on now. You can help with dinner later."

Steve was sitting on the front steps, his shoulders bowed, his arms clasping his knees. He looked up as Micky opened the door. "Ready?"

"Sure!"

They hurried across the lawn and out the front gate. "Ever been to a fish hatchery?" Steve wanted to know.

Micky shook her head.

"There's really not much to see. But it is sort of interesting if you like that sort of thing." He lifted his head. "What do you like to do?"

"Why, I—I—"

His eyes widened in amazement. "You mean you don't know?" he asked incredulously.

"Well, I like to read—" Micky floundered. "And sometimes I think I might like to learn to cook."

She fell silent, her thoughts a jumble of confusion. What did she like anyway? Skating? A little, but not much; not since she'd fallen and the awful boy with the freckles had teased her unrelentingly.

Pictures of her other foster homes flickered through her mind. She remembered camping with the Alexanders, learning to crochet from Mom Appleby. But most of all, she remembered the running, the awful feeling of not really belonging, of searching for something—she wasn't sure what. And then, when the restless feeling got too bad . . . she'd just take off. . . .

I'm sorry, Micky, Mrs. Morton, her caseworker had explained. *There isn't any way we're going to keep you out of the juvenile home if you keep running off.*

Then Loretta had come . . .

"Well," Steve interrupted her thoughts. "What else?"

"What else what?"

"What else do you like to do?" he repeated.

"I don't know." Micky's thoughts twisted in her head. "What about you? What do you like?"

Steve picked up a rock and tossed it in the air. "Lots of things," he said airily, "like swimming, fishing, comics. I even like school."

"I don't," Micky said flatly.

"That's stupid. You have to go, so you might as well like it."

Her fear of new schools, new faces, rose inside her. Would she always be on the fringes, never quite belonging?

"School hasn't been much fun for me," she muttered. "I've been in lots of them and I've never, ever seemed to fit."

She searched for words to explain the paralyzing fear that gripped her every time she stepped onto a new campus. But no words came.

She stamped her foot instead, disturbing the gravel. "I'm not going back."

"I'll bet Dad and Mom say you do," Steve countered.

Micky shrugged. "Maybe I'll just leave. And this time I'll find a way to disappear—" But even as she said it, she wondered. There was something about the Middletons. Her wish to be their daughter intensified each day she was with them.

"We're here!" Steve exclaimed. He pointed to a large cement pond encircled by a metal mesh fence. "This is the adult holding tank."

Micky stopped at the edge, peering into the water.

"I can't see anything—oh, yes, I can! They're big, aren't they?"

"Come on over here!" Steve called. He stood beside the waist-high concrete runways, motioning to her. "This is the spawning channel."

Micky followed and stood beside him. "I can see them better here," she observed.

Steve hurried on to another runway. "This is where they keep the smaller ones."

Micky ran over to him. "Oh," she murmured, "what cute little things." She felt a great urge to lean over the edge and let the silver-colored fish swim between her fingers.

"Look there," Steve gestured toward a young man walking briskly on the steel grate walkway between the holding tanks.

With simple rhythm the man dipped his hand into the bucket, then tossed fish food over the water. The water dimpled with movement. Then dip, toss, dip, toss, and more sparkling dimples. He quit tossing the food as he came up to them, his quick glance darting questioningly to Micky. He extended the bucket toward her. "Would you like to feed the fish?"

Micky drew in a quick, excited breath. "Please." She pulled a handful of coarse fish food from the bucket and tossed it into the tank that held the baby silver. Immediately the water bubbled with action.

"They're so fast," Micky marveled, "and so little. I can hardly believe it!"

"Micky, this is my friend, Jim," Steve explained. "Jim, this is Micky, my . . . new sister."

Reluctantly, Micky broke her attention away from the water and looked at the man Steve had introduced. Faded blue jeans and a brown khaki shirt made him almost blend with the gray concrete and the brownish water. But his blue eyes that contrasted so sharply with his dark beard and hair brimmed with questions. The line between his brows deepened as he asked, "Your new sister?"

"Yep," Steve responded. "She's only been here five days, so she's really new—even if she is three years older than I am!"

A wistful sadness clouded Jim's eyes. His nose twitched suddenly and he glanced down, almost shyly.

Like a rabbit, Micky thought.

There was an awkward pause. She gestured nervously toward the pink house. "I'm living there now," she said.

Jim looked up. "So, you're the new daughter of the house," he mused.

Something in the tone of his voice made sadness well up in Micky. She didn't know what to say. She was glad when Steve came to her rescue.

"I'd like to show Micky where you keep the newly-hatched babies. She's never been inside a hatchery before."

Jim nodded slowly. Once again, Micky was sure she saw his nose twitch. Then he smiled and the rabbit illusion disappeared.

"I'll take you through as soon as I finish the feeding. Okay if I meet you in the lounge in about ten minutes?"

Micky and Steve nodded. "We'll look around outside first," Steve said.

Jim tossed another handful of food over the water. Once again the magical ripples dipped and swirled.

What a strange man he is, Micky thought. *So sad and wistful . . . and the intense way he looked at me!* Had she reminded him of someone he'd known before—someone who might have caused him pain?

She found herself wishing she could learn more about him. It surprised her a little. She didn't often think about other people and their troubles.

"He's different," she said, "different—but nice."

Steve stared at her. "Now don't start going all-girl and getting goo-gaw over him!"

"I'm not!" Micky cried indignantly. She giggled suddenly. "How old is he anyway?"

Steve shrugged. "He must be close to thirty. He's been to college, and he told me once that it took him extra time because he worked his way through."

"College! To feed fish?"

Steve gave her a withering look. "For goodness sake, that isn't all he does! He majored in fishery. That takes five years! And I happen to know he has a girl friend in California. He told me about her once."

Micky tossed her head. "Well, they must not be much in love. If it were me, he wouldn't be up here in Oregon and me down there in California, that's for sure!"

"For crying out loud! You must be falling for him!"

A ripple of laughter bubbled to Micky's lips. "Of course I'm not! I was just thinking that if I were in love, I'd stick close. 'Peter Rabbit' isn't my type anyway, but someday there might be somebody who is."

"Peter Rabbit! Who's Peter Rabbit?"

"Oh," Micky said loftily, "your friend, Jim. The way he twitches his nose and sort of lowers his eyes."

A startled awareness leaped into Steve's eyes. "You know," he said thoughtfully, "he does, doesn't he?"

"And I don't mean it badly, either. It's just that people remind me of animals sometimes. I went to school once with a girl who reminded me of a little field mouse."

"What do I remind you of?"

"I don't know. It doesn't always come. But I think your father is rather like a lion. He roars—and growls, too.

"And courage; he has courage."

"I wouldn't know about that. But come on. I want to look at that tank over there."

"They're called runways," Steve corrected.

Micky nodded. "The fish must be segregated according to size," she noted, "then put in different tanks—runways, I mean."

At the hatchery entrance, Jim opened the door. They went at once to a big, cool room where the outer walls were stacked with gray trays.

Jim gestured toward the trays. "The eggs are kept there."

Micky peered inside a tray. "They look like soft-boiled beads," she said, shuddering. She turned to the long green runways in the middle of the room. "This is more interesting."

It was a fascinating world she peered into. Minute baby fish swam in their own protected world, away from natural predators.

Even Jim seemed different inside these walls. His shyness vanished as he spoke with quiet assurance.

"We've been doing something comparatively new here this year. We've discovered that when we raise the water temperature slightly during the winter months, it speeds their growth."

Micky touched the water with an exploring finger. The tiny fish scattered like droplets of water. "Do many of them die?"

"Not really. We do have to fight a kidney disease that takes some of the older ones." He shook his head. "A fish has a million enemies, but the worst of all is man. For example, poaching is a big problem in this creek."

Steve sounded excited. "Every day, all summer, when the creek is closed to anglers, the state police park, get out, and walk along the bank."

Jim nodded. "We owe our state police a lot of thanks. It's impossible for the hatchery personnel to protect the stream alone. And poaching isn't the only problem."

"Pollution?" Micky asked.

"Yes. Keeping the stream well stocked is our number one job, but keeping the stream clean is everybody's job. We need more people to be aware of what pollutes a stream and reduces our fish population."

On the way back to the house, Steve and Micky talked about it.

"It almost makes you want to get involved," Micky remarked.

"I already am," Steve said confidently. "That's what I'll be studying in college."

"College!" Micky exclaimed. "But you're not even in high school yet."

Steve shrugged. "Doesn't matter. High school offers a lot—biology, chemistry . . ." He raised his eyebrows and looked at her. "It helps to know where you're going."

Sudden shame welled up in Micky as she stared at Steve, the thin stick of a boy with pale blue-gray eyes—not really very sure of himself, she'd thought. His words made her feel almost guilty.

Here she was, three years older, and all she thought

about was running away and—boys.

She looked past Steve and saw someone coming toward them, bright head held high, a fishing pole in hand.

Micky's heart skipped a beat. *Joel.* What would she say to him or he to her? Or would he say nothing because Kent had yelled at him? Micky stopped and waited.

4

Margot

*B*ut it wasn't Joel. Instead, it was a girl who looked amazingly like him.

She had his bright hair, the same lift to the chin, the long body. Even her shoulders were broad and moved with simple grace in response to her long strides.

Micky stared. The girl walked easily, as though she was accustomed to rough country roads. How poised she was, how elegant!

Then the girl smiled, a kind smile, her lips tinted a soft pink. Her smile deepened and Micky forgot her apprehension.

"You must be Micky. Joel asked me to come and . . . see firsthand if you were okay. No pneumonia, huh?"

Micky shook her head. Then the girl smiled at Steve, who awkwardly ground the toe of his shoe into the road.

"How does it feel to have a sister?"

"It's okay," Steve muttered. He sidled toward the edge of the road, obviously anxious to get on with his own affairs.

Quickly Micky came to his rescue. "Thanks a lot for showing me around the hatchery, Steve. Maybe I can return the favor."

Steve nodded and shot off like over-warm Coke popping a bottle cap.

"He's at the age where he doesn't like girls." The girl who looked so much like Joel smiled again at Micky. "He acts like he likes you, though."

"I think he does a little." Micky didn't explain that it was only since her mishap in the creek that he'd begun to warm to her. Instead she said, "You must be Joel's older sister."

"No—younger by a year. I'm Tam—for Tamera. I hope we can be friends, Micky." She gestured with a long, graceful hand. "I could never have too many."

Me either, Micky wanted to say. But she didn't. Friends had been in short supply. She looked at Tamera speculatively. Could this long-legged, sure creature be the hazy outline she'd visualized in the upstairs bedroom? Why not? She was Joel's sister, wasn't she? And Joel was, well—already she sensed he was somebody special.

She had a sudden longing to take the girl up the steep stairs to see her hidden room. If only Loretta . . .

She turned to Tam shyly. "Would you like to come home with me? Loretta fixed me a room."

"Love it." Tam smiled. "Is your room pink like the outside of the house?" she asked curiously.

Micky stopped, startled. "How did you know?"

"I didn't." Tam laughed and took Micky's arm. "I was only guessing. Let's run!"

Both girls were breathless when Micky opened the door to her room. "Why, it's lovely!" Tam exclaimed. She collapsed on the bed and looked around. "But it doesn't look much like you, does it?"

"No—o. Not at all."

Tam locked both hands behind her head, tilting it

thoughtfully to one side. "Rooms should, you know—look like their owners. But of course Loretta didn't know you when she decorated this, did she?"

Micky shook her head. "What do you think would suit me?"

"I'm not exactly sure. I don't know you very well yet. But I don't think you're the fluttering feminine type. This room needs someone who's a little bit fragile, maybe—"

Micky leaned forward. "Would wood paneling and Indian blankets and rag rugs suit me better?"

Tam smiled. "Is that what you like?"

"Yes. And lots of windows to let the outside in. This room is so closed up it gives me the creeps." She gestured toward the curtained window. "All you can see is the backside of the garage."

"Maybe you can change it. New curtains or something. Or would that hurt Loretta's feelings?"

"I'm not sure. I might ask."

They chatted on for some time, content to get acquainted. Then Tam sat up, glancing at her watch. "I should go now, Micky. I'll come again, if it's all right."

"All right?" Micky exclaimed. "It would be wonderful! I don't know anybody around here at all."

"Well, you know me now," Tam said. She got up, stretching like a lazy cat.

After she left, Micky mulled over their conversation. *She acts like she likes me,* she marveled. *She really does. Oh, if only I could have the room upstairs!*

On impulse, Micky went in search of Loretta. She found her downstairs sorting the contents of the hall closet.

Loretta held up a blue denim jacket, obviously too

small for anyone in the family. "Why do I keep such things?" she wondered aloud.

"Loretta—" Micky said uncertainly.

Loretta put the jacket down and looked at her. "What is it, Micky?"

Micky licked her lips. "It's about my room—"

"What about it?"

"I—I don't know exactly. It just doesn't seem to fit."

"Fit?"

"Fit me." Micky searched for the right words. "It's all very lovely . . . too lovely for me. I'm not like that."

Loretta ran her fingers through her dark hair. "I don't think I understand, Micky."

"It isn't easy to explain," Micky said. "It's not that I don't appreciate it—it just isn't me."

"What is you, then, do you think?"

"Something plain—and open. My room is closed up like—like a coffin!" She stopped as a pained look crossed Loretta's face. "I'm sorry," she whispered. "I didn't mean to be ungrateful."

"It's all right, Micky," Loretta said softly. She looked at the clothes piled on the floor, seeming not to see them. "Let's go upstairs. We need to talk."

A tightness like a vise gripped Micky's throat as she followed Loretta up the stairs and into the pink room. Sudden tears blurred her eyes. She hadn't meant to hurt Loretta.

Loretta pulled the white wicker chair close as Micky sank onto the bed. "There's something I need to tell you, Micky. It's painful, and I never thought I'd need to bring it up again. But—this room belonged to Margot, my stepdaughter."

A faraway look veiled Loretta's eyes. "She was a

lovely girl, much like you, Micky, with dark hair and eyes. And no, she wasn't fragile and feminine, either. That was only my dream. She was something else— strong-willed, vibrant, popular with the boys, even though she was only fifteen.

"I let her go swimming that day against my better judgment. She told me she was meeting her girl friend and that they were going to the whale rock up the creek. I never dreamed she would go alone.

"Her brother, Jamie, was in the woods when she cried for help. He came quickly, but he panicked—"

"Loretta, you don't have to tell me—"

"Yes, I do, Micky. You've come into an unhappy family, and it's only right that you know. You're so much like her . . . yet so different. . . .

"We lost Jamie the same day. His father blamed him for not jumping in after Margot. Perhaps if he had, he could have saved her. We'll never know. He ran for help instead."

"What happened to him?"

"Kent went into one of his black rages. Jamie was barely eighteen, but Kent couldn't control his grief. He lashed out at Jamie instead.

"I think Kent was ashamed of him. Jamie was so different from his father. Quiet, gentle, unsure of himself. He had . . . drifting hands . . . that don't take hold—"

Loretta gestured with her own hands, a helpless gesture that twisted Micky's heart. "We never saw Jamie again. I think Kent hurt him too much. And Kent wouldn't go after him. So there we were, left alone, Kent and I and four-year-old Steve.

"I wanted to make it up to Kent by having a daughter to take Margot's place, but it never happened. I was depressed for months. Two of our children—both gone."

Micky blinked hard. "Is that why you wanted me?"

"In a way, maybe. But it's been nine years now, Micky. One can never go back. Not really."

Loretta stood up and walked to the dressing table. She fingered the pink tulle. "This room hasn't been used much since Margot died. Most of the time it's been closed and we tried to forget . . ."

"But what made you—"

Loretta turned, her smile gentle. "I needed a girl," she said simply. "When I saw you, I knew you were the one. . . . Now, about this room. What would you like to do? Fresh paint, wallpaper, new curtains?"

Micky took a long, deep breath. "Do you think I could make it look a little like the room at the top of the stairs? The Indian blanket—"

Loretta's fingers suddenly clenched the fragile pink material, her knuckles turning white. "You were up there?" she asked. "Why, Kent . . . Kent—"

"I climbed up the tree and went in through the window," Micky confessed. "I'm sorry."

"Just don't tell Kent! He gave strict orders that the room be left alone after Jamie left."

Micky stared at her uncomprehendingly. "But why?"

"I think it was because deep down he thought Jamie would change—come home someday—"

"Then I won't be able—"

"No, Micky. You know Kent—or do you? He gets one idea in his head, and he never gives it up."

A shiver ran up Micky's arms; she remembered a shouting, angry man glowering in rage, standing on the creek bank. *But he was hurting,* she thought with sudden understanding. *He was seeing Margot, not me, under the water.*

"But we can paint this room," Loretta offered. "I'll talk to Kent about it." She turned at the door, smiling. "Start planning your colors."

Micky leaned back, pushing the pillow into a comfortable lump under her head. But she wasn't thinking about colors. She was thinking about Loretta. Once more her eyes examined the room's details. She also saw an uncertain young stepmother planning ruffled curtains, selecting dainty pink fabric and fragile ribbons.

And she saw something else. She saw two hurting parents who had in one day lost two children. Micky shivered and turned onto her stomach, burying her face in the pillow.

That afternoon clouds built up, obscuring the pale spring sunshine. Micky slipped into a jacket and hurried outdoors, eager to get better acquainted with the creek before the rain began.

She sped across the lawn as Steve came in the gate.

"Hi!" she called. "Where've you been?"

He grinned as he latched the gate. "Talking to Jim. I even got to help him a little while—"

The door to the house opened and Kent came toward them. There was a dark thundering look on his face, and Micky caught her breath. Had she somehow made him angry?

"Steve!" Kent roared. "Where have you been?"

Steve dropped his chin. He scraped the toe of his shoe against the cement walk. "At—at the hatchery. I was helping—"

Kent tossed him a withering look. "What do you mean *helping*? You were supposed to be cleaning out the garage! I told you earlier and off you went!" He slammed his fist into his palm. "When I give you a job to do, I expect you to do it! How do you ever expect to amount to anything if you don't learn responsibility at home?"

"I was going to! But I thought—"

"The trouble is, you don't think!"

But Steve was already scuttling to the garage. A lump swelled up in Micky's throat. Why couldn't Kent see the light that shone from Steve's eyes when he talked about the hatchery—about Jim?

She opened her mouth for an angry retort, then clamped it shut. This was no time to get between a father and son.

———

By evening the rain had begun. All night it lashed at Micky's window, driven by a wind that moaned through the fir trees.

Once she wakened to the far-off sound of voices— arguing voices, pained voices. *Kent,* she thought, *Loretta.* Then, *Margot . . . Jamie . . .*

Micky shoved her head beneath the pillow and tried to go back to sleep. The wind and rain, instead of lulling her, roused unhappy memories.

She saw her self of long ago: a small girl with blazing eyes, shouting at another child. "Don't call me Michelle! I'm Micky. Only my mama calls me Michelle."

And then the awful hurt—her mother gone.

Her mother's face, almost forgotten now, floated unbidden into Micky's mind, her long dark hair blowing in the wind. Micky had last seen her driving off in a battered station wagon, her two brothers tucked in front, the back loaded with suitcases and boxes.

Then descending darkness—her mother was gone, really gone.

Then Micky saw another face—it was Margot—strikingly attractive, her dark eyes sparkling with mischief and life.

Resolutely, Micky pushed the image aside, but it returned, Margot's eyes teasing. "Come on!" she shouted, and she shoved Micky beneath the cold water of the rushing stream—

Micky jerked awake, drenched in cold sweat, wondering how long she'd been asleep. She looked at the clock—*4:30.*

Determined to sleep, she shoved the faces aside and thought of a huge white cherry tree that grew and grew until she was lost in its branches. . . .

When she wakened, the house was quiet. She felt a sudden urgency to see the cherry tree, to touch its blossoms.

She jumped out of bed, grabbing her white terry robe. Barefoot, she slipped down the stairs and out through the basement entrance.

The great white tree lowered its wet, sweet-scented branches toward her. Gently, Micky pulled one close to her nose.

The quiet squeak of the door hinge made her turn. Kent Middleton stood in the doorway, his legs braced apart, his arms folded. He cleared his throat uneasily.

"Loretta said you'd like to move into the room upstairs," he said. "You may do so whenever you wish."

The cherry branch jerked upward as Micky released it and flew toward Kent. "Oh, Mister—" she cried. "Thank you. Thank you!"

Then Kent's arms were around her. He awkwardly patted her shoulder. "Now, now. You just run on back and start moving your things. I've already unlocked the door."

Breathlessly, Micky disengaged herself from his embrace. "Oh, Mister Middleton—"

"You can call me Kent," he said. "And if that doesn't suit you, Uncle Kent will do." He turned and walked toward the stream, a lonely figure, his shoulders squared and rigid.

"Uncle Kent," Micky murmured. "My very own *Uncle* Kent." Then she was racing up the stairs two at a time.

"Loretta!" she cried. "I get to move upstairs, right now, today!"

The iron skillet in Loretta's hand clattered onto the stove. "Why, Micky!" she gasped. "Did Kent really—" Micky pressed her hands together and nodded. "He told me just now. I can move in right away! And—he said I could call him Uncle Kent."

To Micky's surprise, Loretta covered her face with her hands.

"Loretta?" Micky whispered uncertainly. "I—if you'd rather I didn't . . ."

"No, no. It isn't that." She lowered her hands and smiled tremulously. "There's nothing I'd like better than to have that room used. It's been like a tomb—a silent reminder . . ."

She put her hand on Micky's shoulder. "To think . . ." she marveled, "he asked you to call him Uncle Kent. Perhaps—after nine years—some healing has begun."

5

The Spirit of the Stream

*M*icky and Loretta stood in the middle of the upstairs room, and Loretta glanced around it.

"It's going to need a thorough cleaning, with plenty
of soap and water," Loretta stated flatly, wrinkling her
nose. "But first let's empty the closet."

Memories of the tiny wooden deer and the old
scrapbook urged Micky to volunteer, "Let me. I'll put
everything in a box, and you can go through it later—"

Loretta nodded and stepped to the window. The
rain pounded against it, and she drew her finger across
the glass.

"You'll need window cleaner too . . ." Her gaze
drifted to the desk, "and furniture polish . . ."

"I can do everything," Micky said eagerly.

Loretta smiled. "Of course." She moved to the bed.
"I'll bring up fresh sheets—more blankets." She pulled
on the edge of the bright Indian blanket. "You like this
one, huh?"

"Love it!" Micky exclaimed. She felt a sudden de-
sire for Loretta to leave the room, so she could taste
alone the joy of having her own place. "Could I start
right away?"

Loretta meandered around the room, lightly touching the furniture and wall decor. She leaned against the

window frame again and watched the rain sluicing against the pane.

"The creek is on the rise," she said. "If this rain keeps on, the steelhead will move upstream."

"Why?" Micky wondered aloud.

"They like the high water. Fishermen lie awake praying for it." Loretta turned from the window.

Please go! Micky pleaded silently. *I want to be alone.*

With a last glance around, Loretta reached for the door. "I'll get what you need, Micky. There're boxes in the garage—"

Impulsively, Micky covered Loretta's hand with her own. "Thank you."

Loretta shrugged. "Thank *you*, Micky. And I think Jamie would thank you, too. This room needs to be occupied, not locked up like a tomb."

"What about Margot's room? What will you do with it?" Micky blurted.

"Before you came we used it for guests. I'd like to redecorate it—maybe. But I really have no heart for it." Loretta sighed deeply. "If you have any ideas . . ."

After Loretta left, Micky opened the closet. The remainders of a lost boyhood greeted her: a battered baseball mitt, a bat propped in the corner, the old scrapbook.

"Steve might like these," Micky murmured, pulling them onto the floor. She reached for the carved deer, turning it in her hands.

It's lovely, she thought, *so fragile—so real-looking.* Her fingers caressed its pricked ears, the graceful neck. Thoughtfully, she put it with the mitt and bat. She pulled out a mesh bag of marbles, then another small wooden carving. This one was of a fox, its head bent low, as if scuttling through the brush, away from an enemy.

I wonder if Jamie carved these? Micky mused. *But they're so perfect.* She set the fox beside the deer and reached up to the back of the shelf. Her fingertips brushed something large and ungainly.

She pulled out an exquisitely carved totem pole, about two feet tall. Micky traced the outlines of a beaver and a deer with her fingers. At the top of the carving, a large eagle had been freed from the wood. Its fierce eyes glared at her; its wings spread wide, almost threatening, yet protecting too.

"The spirit of the creek," Micky muttered unconsciously.

Excitement rose within her as she examined the base of the pole. There was a slim trout, a crayfish, a nymph . . .

"Oh!" she cried as she discerned a water skipper astride the clearly defined water surface. Then, "A dragonfly! Its tail is in the water. It must be laying eggs. And a fallen leaf . . ."

She turned the pole in her hands, marveling at the unique workmanship.

After a while, Micky set it beside the bat and stepped back. "You don't belong here," she said. "You should be sitting on a rock high above the creek."

Suddenly she wanted to share her find with Loretta. As she headed for the stairs, her feet seemed to stop of their own accord. Doubts flashed in her mind. Was this the right thing to do?

She decided against it. Loretta had been hurt so much already. She would pack the totem pole into a box with the rest of Jamie's things and say nothing.

But the pole looked out of place stashed awkwardly among sweaters and the odd collection of Jamie's treasures.

Micky carefully replaced the totem pole on the shelf in the closet. She hesitated briefly, then put the fox and deer beside it. The old scrapbook followed. Later she would decide what to do with them. Only the box of clothes and a few odds and ends would find their way downstairs.

Micky spent the remainder of the day cleaning. The rain slacked off a bit toward evening, and she was amazed to see a dozen or more fishermen converge on the stream. She leaned out her window, eager to see if Joel might be among them. But there was no sight of the curly, reddish brown hair or the shoulders that moved with their peculiar grace.

Micky wakened the next morning to a whirl of activity. The kitchen table was cluttered with cornflakes, toast crumbs, and sticky strawberry-jam knives. Kent had already gone, and Loretta stood by the stove, buttering a piece of toast.

"You'll have to fix something for yourself," she said. "It's my morning to work at the pharmacy." She gestured toward the stove. "If you could put the potatoes in the oven at four-thirty and make a salad, I'd appreciate it. I can do the rest when I get home." She went out the kitchen door, her toast in hand.

"It's always like this the day Mom works," Steve grumbled from the doorway. "I hate fixing my own breakfast!"

He too disappeared, but he was back a few minutes later lugging a pile of books, which he flopped onto the table.

He eyed Micky curiously. "Think you can stand it around here by yourself for a whole day?" he asked.

Micky shrugged. She almost wished she'd waited to move into her new room. But it was too late for that. She'd already spent her first night in the special retreat, a night of listening to tossing firs and rain, the roar of the stream. She peered out the kitchen window.

"Won't this rain ruin the cherry blossoms?" she asked pensively. But Steve was already running out to catch a ride up the hill with an obliging neighbor.

The day dragged worse than Micky had imagined it could. After she had cleaned the kitchen, scrubbed the potatoes, and planned what to have for a salad, there was nothing else to do.

Or was there? The creek outside roared its invitation.

Micky shrugged into a hooded sweatshirt and hurried to meet it. Swollen with the rains, darkened with run-off, it no longer sang sweetly.

But Micky didn't mind. A strange excitement filled her as she faced the wind and felt the spray on her face.

She crossed the bridge below the hatchery and walked down the other side of the creek. Mossy vine maples mingled with drooping cedars. Tall sword ferns brushed her jeans.

The stream fascinated her. It roared and raced over huge rocks. Like a mighty giant, it pushed an occasional limb along and drew small sticks into its current, propelling them downstream.

Micky went around the bend, parting the bushes as she walked. And suddenly there before her stood Joel on a log jutting into the stream. He turned.

"Micky!" he exclaimed. He balanced carefully, then ran lightly toward her.

"I thought you were in school," Micky blurted uncertainly.

"Got out at noon. Teacher's workday." He looked at her intently. "What're you up to?"

Ignoring his question, she said, "The creek . . . it looks so different."

Joel nodded. "It's in its wild mood now. I love it this way." He grinned. "It's sort of exciting, isn't it?"

"Yes, it is." She changed the subject. "I looked for you yesterday. I thought you might be fishing—many were out."

Joel shook his head. "Sunday is a family day at our house. We go to church in the morning—and in the evening."

"Really?" Micky looked at him with open curiosity. "Why?"

"Why?" Joel's green eyes regarded her steadily. "Because Jesus Christ is an important part of our lives . . . of my life—"

"Wow!" Micky exclaimed. She picked up a stick and tossed it into the swirling current. "I've never been inside a church in my life—and Jesus Christ? I've never given Him much thought at all."

"Want to come to church with me?" Joel asked.

Micky squatted on the ground, resting her elbows on her knees, carefully balancing on her toes. "I don't know," she said. She looked up. "What do you do there?"

"We study the Bible in our Sunday school class, then we sing and listen to what Pastor Briggs has to say about God's Word. It's cool."

"Cool?"

Joel got down beside her, his fingers busy peeling a small twig. "Church is special to me, Micky. It's my family. And that's where Jesus Christ comes into it. He's our God, our Lord, and we love Him and serve

Him together. Didn't any of your foster parents or your real mom and dad ever take you to church?"

Micky shook her head. "Mom Appleby used to go. But she always said she wouldn't force religion down anybody's throat. So I never went. Someday maybe I'll go with you. But not right now." She leaped to her feet. "Look, Joel! There, up the creek—it looks like an animal caught in the current."

Joel looked in the direction of her pointing finger. "Let's go!" he exclaimed. He began to run, and Micky followed, over the rocks, across the jutting roots.

As they got closer, she realized it was a young doe caught in the swirling waters. "Oh, the poor thing!" she cried, "Will she die?"

Joel didn't answer. As the deer struggled helplessly, Micky could detect the fear in her dark, liquid eyes. The animal reminded her of the carving Jamie had done. She caught her breath.

"I'm going in after her!" Joel exclaimed.

He plunged into the water and waded to the middle of the stream. As he drew closer, Micky could see the panic increase in the deer's eyes.

"Oh, beautiful lady," Micky whispered. "You are the spirit of the creek. Don't be afraid—"

As Joel reached the deer, both hands touched her neck, then went beneath the water.

"She's caught on a log," he shouted. "I can't budge her—"

"I'll come," Micky called. The icy water splashed around her ankles, and she shuddered.

"Wait—" Joel cried, "go for help—"

But Micky kept on. The water rose high on her legs, then to her waist. Her foot caught on a rock, and she staggered forward, gasping as the water rose nearly chest-deep. Joel's hand reached out to her, and for an instant she clung tightly. Then she was beside him.

"If you could push down the limb while I shove on her rear, I think we can get her free."

Micky obliged. The limb was deep and she was wet to her neck, but she didn't care. The lovely doe's face was close to her own.

"Don't be afraid," she whispered, "we're here to help." Was that a flicker of trust she saw?

She gulped a mouthful of water, then shoved hard on the branch, suddenly conscious of Joel's hand touching hers. The deer moved, and Micky lurched backward. She clutched the submerged log, catching herself.

Joel's face was close to hers. "All right?"

Micky nodded. She put her arms around the deer's neck and began to pull her toward the shore. Joel pushed on the animal's withers, speaking encouraging words. The young doe's hooves struck the rocks. Together they lifted her onto the shore, but her spindly legs couldn't hold her; she took one step forward and collapsed.

Joel and Micky looked at each other.

"Phone the hatchery," Joel gasped, pushing his soaked hair off his forehead.

Micky nodded numbly, turned, and stumbled forward. Her clothes clung to her, hampering her stride.

Moments later she burst through the basement door of the house, muddy footsteps trailing her up the stairs and into the kitchen. Her trembling fingers traced down the numbers.

"We just pulled a deer out of the creek—" she explained through chattering teeth. "It's alive—"

"And who is *we*?" a courteous male voice asked.

"We're the pink house just below you. We—"

"I'll send the manager right away. Wait there."

Micky put the receiver down, her thoughts tumbling. *First, change clothes; second, grab a blanket to cover the deer; third, bring a jacket of Kent's for Joel.* She rushed up the stairs.

She peeled her clothes off into a soaking heap on her bedroom floor. She dressed again quickly, then pulled the extra blanket from her bed. As she hurried downstairs, she grabbed a denim jacket from the hall closet.

She was out the door in time to meet Jim. He stood there awkwardly, ill-at-ease, worry lines crinkling around his dark blue eyes. "You're—you're the manager?" Micky asked, unable to hide the amazement in her voice.

"No—they just sent me. The manager's off the grounds." A sudden smile relieved the frown lines on his forehead. "Now where is this swimming deer of yours?"

"Down the creek. Come on."

Without words the two followed the rushing stream to Joel and the trembling doe lying on the bank. Micky tossed Joel the jacket, then bent over the deer.

"You poor thing," she murmured. Gently she spread the sturdy blanket over the wet, trembling form. "Will she live?"

Joel slipped the denim jacket on. "Not if we leave her here."

Jim nodded. The frown with which he'd met Micky at the door deepened as he ran his fingers through his hair. "If we move her clear up to the hatchery, it'll be hard on her." He looked intently at Micky. "Would it be okay with your folks if we put her in your basement temporarily, where it's warm?"

"Oh, sure!" Micky cried. "That would be just fine."

Joel scowled. "You don't think Kent would get angry?" he asked, looking at Micky.

Courage welled up within her as Micky looked at the frightened deer. "Kent and Loretta won't mind—I'm sure. And I could call them."

"They aren't there?" Jim asked, something like relief flitting across his face.

Micky shook her head. "I'm home alone. But I'll accept the responsibility. Let's get her to our basement."

Without further delay, Jim bent and scooped up the deer, blanket and all.

Joel and Micky exchanged knowing looks. Then suddenly Joel's hand was clasping Micky's. They fell into step behind Jim.

6

A Deer in the Kitchen

"*B*est stand back a bit," Jim advised, "she's a wild creature." Gently he laid the doe on the basement floor.

Micky stepped back, her eyes riveted on the beautiful animal. "Will—will she make it?"

"She's got a good chance. But she's cold, clear through. She needs to warm up. He nodded toward Joel. "So does he."

"Oh," Micky exclaimed. She tore her fascinated gaze from the doe and looked at Joel, tousled hair covering his brows. His jeans clung to him; his jacket showed wet streaks.

He shuddered, grinning through faintly blue lips. "Maybe I could borrow something of Kent's—"

Micky dashed up the stairs. How thoughtless she'd been. . . .

Feeling a ridiculous combination of intruder and shamed child, Micky hurried into Kent and Loretta's bedroom. A girl in a picture frame on the walnut dresser smiled at her. *Margot?* But the face wasn't the face of her dream. This girl had one dimple, and her slightly parted lips had a beckoning, inviting, come-be-with-me look.

Trying not to think about the picture, Micky began

pulling out blue jeans, a sweater, underwear and socks, then returned to the basement.

The color rose into her cheeks as she handed the clothes to Joel. But he took them without comment, stepping into the adjoining bathroom.

Once again Micky looked at the doe. A joyous exhilaration rose within her as she saw those wild, dark eyes, this time clear and unafraid, looking back at her.

Jim looked up. "May I leave her here with you then?" he asked.

Micky nodded. Reluctantly she regarded the man kneeling beside the doe. The strange wistfulness she'd noticed when she'd first met him at the hatchery was lurking in his eyes again. He bent down, smoothing the corner of the blanket.

How beautiful his hands are, Micky marveled suddenly. *Could he be an artist, or a pianist?*

"If anything comes up you can call." Jim rose to his feet. "The most important thing is to not frighten her. As soon as she starts moving around, just open the door." He waved his hand. "She'll be gone in a flash."

After Jim left, Micky sat back on the braided rug and thought about the deer. "You need a name, little one," she murmured, "something beautiful and wild and—free."

"How about 'Morning'?" Joel asked. He plopped down beside her, his wet hair neatly combed, his fresh-scrubbed face sparkling with interest.

"Or 'Fern,' " Micky said, remembering the tall ferns that had brushed her ankles alongside the stream.

Joel nodded. "Ferns are beautiful, wild and free," he agreed.

"But mornings are more unpredictable." Micky smiled at the doe. "I have a feeling she is too."

"So 'Morning' it is." Joel turned to address the deer. "Good afternoon, Morning. Nice having you here."

Micky and Joel smiled at each other, their anxiety over the deer temporarily forgotten. But not for long. Morning suddenly struggled to her feet, stood swaying, then dropped back onto the rug.

"Is she all right?" Micky cried.

A worry line crinkled Joel's forehead. "I . . . think so."

They watched her intently for several minutes. Then Micky heard a door open and close upstairs.

"What's going on in this place?" Kent roared. "There's mud all over the kitchen!"

The doe lurched to her feet; the blanket fell to the floor. Before Joel or Micky could open the outside door, Morning turned and raced for the only escape she could see—up the stairs, her tiny hooves clattering on the steps.

Joe and Micky tore after her. The four of them collided at the top of the stairs—Kent, Morning, Joel, and Micky.

A look of bewildered unbelief crossed Kent's face as the doe shoved her nose into his stomach. "What—"

"Grab her!" Joel cried. But it was too late. Kent had already moved aside.

Her scrambling hooves clattered, then slid on the linoleum floor; her legs splayed. Quickly recovering her balance, she tried to leap. Instead, she collided with a chair, overturning it with a crash.

She scampered onto the carpet in the living room, then stood, poised, ready to leap through the wide picture window.

Joel lunged, grabbing her withers. Then Micky was at her head. "No, no, Morning," she panted.

Together she and Joel shoved the trembling animal through the kitchen and out the utility entrance. At the door they stepped back, releasing her.

The doe stood quietly for a couple of seconds, then in one big graceful arc she was off the front steps and running. The gate was closed, but Morning leaped it without effort. At the woods' edge she stopped and looked back.

Micky was almost certain she detected a flicker of trust in those large dark eyes, even though she was too far away to see for sure. Then Morning flitted her fan-like tail in farewell and was gone, the vine maples gathering her into the forest.

Micky touched Joel's hand. "Do you think we'll ever see her again?"

Joel did not reply, but turned to enter the kitchen again.

"Leave you alone a day and what happens?" Kent roared. "Mud all over the house, a wild deer inside, up-turned furniture!" Suddenly his roar turned into a great laugh. He slapped his knee and said, "I'll never forget it as long as I live . . . that deer sliding across the lino-leum—and you two guiding her out again . . . to free-dom."

He grabbed Joel's hand and shook it vigorously. "I wouldn't have missed it for anything, young man." Then he tousled Micky's dark mop. "You're something else, Micky! Never a dull moment . . ."

He disappeared into the living room mumbling something to himself, leaving the two young people stunned by his uncharacteristic behavior.

"I wonder what he'll say when he realizes I borrowed his clothes for you?" Micky whispered.

A smile creased Joel's lips. He looked down at his baggy jeans. "I have a feeling he already noticed."

For the first time Micky really looked at the over-sized clothes. "Oh, Joel," she gasped. "You do look funny! Those pants and that sweatshirt—"

Suddenly the tenseness and the humor of the situation struck them both. They collapsed onto two kitchen chairs and laughed until tears rolled down their faces.

———

It was there that Loretta found them, the kitchen floor still splotched with mud, the upturned chair.

Joel sobered in a hurry. "Excuse me, Mrs. Middleton," he said, standing. "I—"

Micky caught her breath. "I'm sorry, Loretta. I forgot—"

"It was the deer—" Joel interrupted.

"In the kitchen," Micky explained.

"A deer in the kitchen?" Loretta repeated. "You'll have to do better than that!"

"There really was a deer here, Mrs. Middleton," Joel explained. "Actually, it was in the creek—"

"And by the looks of you two, so were you!"

Joel nodded. "That's right. But we saved the deer. We got her out—"

"And brought her into the basement, where it was warm. But when she heard Kent's voice she panicked and raced up here," Micky continued.

"Micky and I will clean up," Joel volunteered. "We would have done it sooner, but—"

Micky went for the mop and pail. "You just relax, Loretta. We'll take care of everything."

Joel grabbed the mop from Micky's hand.

"I'll put the potatoes in the oven," Micky offered, as Loretta left the room shaking her head.

Joel filled the bucket with hot water. "Boy, what a mess!"

"Yeah, Loretta must be wondering what kind of a girl she got stuck with," Micky murmured.

"Knock it off!" Joel scolded. He had the kitchen mopped in no time and then went to spot-washing the carpet in the living room while Micky chopped vegetables for the salad.

Joel went in search of Kent and was back in a few minutes, a warm fleece-lined jacket draped over his arm. "Kent's a great guy," he remarked. "See you later, Micky."

————

That night at the supper table Micky recounted the afternoon's adventure so Steve could get the whole story.

"Wow!" Steve kept repeating. "And I missed it," he concluded. "Phooey on after-school games!"

Later that evening, Micky took the small deer woodcarving from her room to show Loretta.

She sat with an open book on her lap and looked up, smiling. The lamp brought out the rich, warm highlights in her hair. "What do you have there?" Loretta asked.

Micky sat down on the footstool beside her and held out the small deer in her hand. "I found this in my room."

Loretta gently took the carving from her and turned it thoughtfully in her hand. "Jamie made this," she said softly.

"I think it's beautiful," Micky breathed. "The details, the lift of her head. It reminds me of Morning."

She glanced around the room. "Could we keep it on the window ledge? I'd like it there to remind me—"

But Loretta shook her head. "I'm sorry, Micky. Even when Jamie was with us, Kent wouldn't let me keep the carvings around." She dropped the small deer into Micky's palm.

"But, why?"

Loretta leaned back and closed her eyes. "Kent's a very different, very intense man, Micky. It's hard for him to change, hard for him to accept differences in others.

"Jamie's carvings showed such promise—the work of a born artist. But Kent couldn't see it. He thought they were worthless."

"But they aren't!" Micky protested.

Loretta opened her eyes. A slight smile flitted across her face. "Of course they aren't, Micky. But they didn't represent the kind of son Kent wanted—a strong, masculine-type, one who'd amount to something in this world. To Kent, Jamie was simply making piles of wood chips in the garage." She sighed. "And now Steve tries so hard to measure up. He plays football, soccer—hates every minute of it. He'd rather be poring over books, dreaming over at the hatchery about fish and other wildlife."

She put the book on the table beside her and stood up. "You may have the deer carving, Micky. Just keep it in your room."

Micky looked again at the lovely figure. It was beautiful, but so sad, so very, very sad.

"There's something else in the closet, Loretta," she blurted. "A carved totem pole."

Loretta frowned. "A totem pole? I don't remember anything like that."

"If you want to see it, I'll show you."

Loretta followed Micky up the stairs.

"I put it back into the closet," she explained, opening the door.

Carefully, she lifted it from the shelf and set it on the floor. Loretta looked at it, wonder growing in her eyes. "Why, it's beautiful," she faltered. "But I've never seen it before."

"It was shoved way back on the shelf," Micky said. "It would have been easy to miss."

Loretta got down on her knees, carefully examining the base. "There's trout down here," she said excitedly, "and water skippers." Her hands moved up the pole. "And here's a leaf drifting over the water."

"It represents Eagle Creek, doesn't it?"

Loretta nodded. "I can see the waterline, too. Right here." She bent closer. "Why, Micky, I think . . ."

Loretta laid the pole over her knee and began to twist the base. It opened.

Micky gasped. "Is it hollow?" she whispered.

Loretta peered inside. "Yes, but it's empty. Wait . . . I see something." She pulled out a crumpled piece of paper. "It's a note of some kind," she said in a trembling voice. Her hands shook as she unfolded it.

"It's from Jamie," she whispered, "and it's addressed to the creek." As she scanned the words, her face drained of color. "Oh, Micky," she cried, "the poor boy! The poor, poor child!"

Micky held out her hand. "May I see it?" she asked uncertainly.

Loretta nodded. "Of course. It was written years ago . . . he was really just a child—"

She covered her face in her hands and sobbed.

Before she could read it, Micky dropped the paper and wrapped her arms around Loretta. "I'm sorry," she whispered, "I shouldn't have shown you the pole—"

"No, no, it's not your fault; it was so like my Jamie to write like that," she cried. "And we hurt him so much!"

Micky held her again, awkwardly. She didn't know what to say or do.

When her sobbing subsided, Loretta lifted her head. "I'm sorry, Micky," she said quietly.

Micky swallowed hard. "I'm the one who's sorry," she muttered.

Loretta smiled weakly. "You had no way of knowing, Micky. And I overreacted." She reached for a tissue from the dresser. "I'm going downstairs now. Thanks. I needed to see the letter . . . it helps me to understand things a little better."

When Loretta was gone, Micky picked up the note to read it for herself. Then she hesitated, wondering if she should pry into something so personal, so touching. Then her curiosity overcame her reluctance, and she sat down on the bed and smoothed the paper out.

7

Shouting—Always Shouting

Dear Eagle Creek,

I loved you, but now I hate you; you've taken my sister, the only one who ever really understood.

My father hates me. He loved HER, because she was fire and vigor and wasn't afraid of anything or anybody.

But you took her. You pressed her beneath you, held her down until she had no more breath, and it was all my fault. I should have leaped in after her. But I was afraid and ran. The others came but it was too late! Too late!

Oh, God, forgive me. Will that day be forever in my memory? Mother standing so still, so wooden, not looking at me, not caring. Dad so angry—shouting, always shouting—

Micky's eyes stung with unexpected tears. She knew how Kent's rage could strike fear into hearts. And his own son! How could he?

Pent up anger suddenly spilled out of Micky's own heart. She drove her fist into her pillow again and again.

"I hate him!" she cried. "All he does is yell and rage. He didn't even try to understand Jamie, and now Steve. He should be tarred and feathered—"

Micky interrupted her own outrage. *Should he?*

Somehow he'd inspired love in Loretta. And he had been okay about the deer in the kitchen—even laughed about it.

She thought of that morning beneath the cherry tree when he'd told her she could move into the upstairs room. And he'd told her then she could call him "Uncle Kent." Even though the "Uncle" refused to come from her lips, he'd still said she could.

Micky's anger spent itself as quickly as it came. She picked up Jamie's letter from the floor where it had fallen and read on.

> Once, God, I thought I loved You. But no more.
>
> You're mean—poison mean. I'm running away from you, Eagle Creek. No one cares, not even my family. I'm going far away where no one will ever find me—ever. Jamie
> P.S. Goodbye, Eagle Nest. Goodbye. Maybe someday . . .

The rest of his words were torn from the paper. Micky looked up, her cheeks wet.

"He'll come back," she whispered. "The stream, this home—they'll pull him back."

She stretched out on the bed, bunching the pillow beneath her head. *How strange,* she thought, *the way he mixed God and the creek together.*

The house was still, yet Micky felt that much living had once gone on inside its walls. A boy had run up and down the stairs; a sister and brother had called to each other as they played beneath the birches. There was only quiet now.

Micky was motionless for a long time, staring at the totem pole with a slight frown on her face, eyes narrowed, jaw firm. Her thoughts were confused, disconnected, flitting back to Jamie's note.

Once she said aloud, "God—'poison mean'? I don't know much about Him, but He can't be like that, can He?"

Later, in a puzzled half whisper, "I think Jamie knew God, maybe even like Joel does. But hurt made his thoughts get all mixed up."

Finally, "I wish I could have known Jamie. I really do."

After a while she got up and began to get ready for bed. She pulled on flannel pajamas and brushed her hair until it gleamed. Before she snuggled under the Indian blanket, she picked up the letter, folded it carefully, and put it back inside the totem pole, then placed the totem pole on the window ledge beside the deer and the fox. The three seemed to go together.

The eagle with lowered wings, the timid deer, and the dashing trout watched over that night, flavoring Micky's dreams with a touch of the wild. A running deer came closer—closer. Just as she reached out her hand, it dashed away—only to reappear some distance away, nibbling grass in a field of sun-drenched daisies.

———

In the morning, Micky worked alone in the rain-soaked garden. She vigorously attacked an overgrown bridal wreath bush, hewing it down, digging out its huge roots. Her face became flushed and damp while last year's leaves clung to her flannel shirt and her hands became caked with mud.

After clearing the root hole of old root strands, she shoved dirt into it, smoothing it with a rake. A robin trilled its bewilderment from the cherry tree—or was it anticipating lunch from the soft, damp earth?

Micky found it fun to poke among the frail pansy

plants, then stand back and appraise their altered appearance. A drift of blossoms reminiscent of winter snow blew toward her. Loretta came out of the house just then and they admired the freshly prepared corner together.

After a warm, sudsy shower and a hot soup lunch, Micky rambled down to the creek. A great curiosity rose in her as she fingered green lichens and caressed great shaggy mosses. Was the message of Jamie's carvings changing her? Or was it the note he left that caused her to see things in a different light?

Micky wasn't sure. She only knew that something deep inside her seemed to have been kindled into flame. She had to learn about crayfish and goldfinches, robins and deer, mayflowers and trilliums.

———

She tried to express herself that night when the family gathered for supper in the warm kitchen.

Loretta looked up. "Lichens?" she asked. "What about them?"

"I'd just like to find out more about how they grow, what they're called. And the stream life—the little nymphs and the dragonflies. I found some big white bumpy things growing on a log, too. I wondered what they were."

"Conches," Steve explained. "They're parasites."

"You sure do know your biology," Micky said with some astonishment. "I've never heard of conches."

"I like science, and our teacher knows all about the plants and animals in the local forests."

"Anyway," Micky continued, "I also saw a bird flitting around in the vine maples. I'd never seen one like it before. It had a red head, and it appeared to be looking for something."

"We have the *Audubon* and the *National Geographic* magazines," Steve told her. "You can learn a lot from them. I'll show them to you after dinner."

Kent put down his fork. "They teach that sort of thing at the high school here," he explained. "When you start this fall you ought to check into some of those courses."

School—of course she knew she'd have to go back. The thought made knots roll up in her stomach. Why did Kent have to mention it now? She'd only be a junior when she should be a senior.

Her caseworker's words rang in her mind. *Because it's so close to year's end and you're so far behind, we recommend you stay out until fall. A new start would be good for you.*

And it was my running off that did it, Micky thought, *my sheer stupidity*. Her face burned.

Loretta was steering the conversation into smoother channels. "They have bird and tree identification books at the library in town. Maybe that would help. We could stop there some afternoon."

Steve looked at Micky intently. "I could bring you some from the school library, too."

Micky mumbled her thanks and excused herself.

———

Later that evening she was pleasantly surprised to answer a knock at the door and find Tam's smiling face.

The two girls sat on the living room carpet, Steve's *National Geographic*s spread around them, their Coke bottles positioned precariously close by.

"Do they really have classes at school that tell you

about things like trees, plants, wildflowers, and wild-life?" Micky asked her friend.

"Well, that's not really my specialty," Tam said, sipping her Coke. "But Joel took biology last year. He had a lot of fun making a wildflower scrapbook with pressed flowers. I remember some of his diagrams of plant parts, too.

"Now me, I'm more into fun things, like ceramics and home economics." She looked thoughtful. "You know, Micky, you and Joel sort of like the same things."

Micky pulled a magazine closer. "Look at this picture of Mt. St. Helens!" she exclaimed. "Isn't it spectacular?"

But Tam wasn't paying attention. "I wish you'd go to church with us," she said unexpectedly.

Micky put the magazine down. "Why?"

Tam set her Coke beside her. "I think Joel would like to date you," she confided, "but he's got this idea that he can't because you're not a Christian." She tossed her head. "I'm a Christian too, but I don't feel quite that way. I'd date a fellow who wasn't a believer if I knew his moral standards were the same as mine—" She smiled at Micky. "And I know you're a good person, Micky."

The memory of her rage at Kent's treatment of his sons exploded in Micky's mind. "Oh, no . . . no, I'm not, Tam."

Tam's eyebrows lifted inquiringly, but Micky was silent. The roar of the creek outside was more noticeable when they weren't talking.

"Maybe I should—" she said after a moment.

"Should what?"

"Go to church." She changed the subject abruptly. "Now these are the kind of pictures I go for; close-ups of tiny things. See those red and black ants, and the round bright eyes on that jumping spider?"

After a while Tam left, but Micky lingered over the magazines. The bustling world of life on a rock ledge captivated her imagination. What tiny creatures live there! It would be that way at the creek, too, only different. . . .

Loretta brought her back to reality. "Telephone, Micky!"

Micky, a magazine still clutched in her hand, hurried into the kitchen. She picked up the receiver.

"Micky, it's me, Joel—What are you doing?"

"Right now?" She giggled suddenly. "I'm talking to you—but I was looking at magazines. Steve gave me a stack of *National Geographic*s and some old copies of the *Audubon*."

"Good, aren't they? But what I was calling about—would you like to go with Tam and me to the May Day celebration at our high school? It's always sort of special, with marching bands and Maypole dances. It would give you a chance to meet the kids, too."

May Day celebration—marching bands—with Joel?

Tam's words intruded into her wildly spinning thoughts. *I think Joel would like to date you, but he's got this idea he can't because you're not a Christian.*

"I—I . . ." Micky started.

I wish you'd go to church with us, Tam had said. *I know you're a good person, Micky.*

"Are you there, Micky?" Joel asked.

"Yes, yes, of course. I was just thinking. I'd like that. And Joel—do you suppose you could pick me up

Sunday morning so I could go to church with you and Tam?"

Afterward Micky wondered why she'd said it. But it was too late now. She was committed. Somehow, deep inside, she was glad.

8

People Are More Important

"*T*am said a dress," Micky muttered as she got ready for church. She pushed several hangers in her closet aside, carefully examining each outfit.

There weren't many; a slimming navy blue that made her dark hair look darker, a soft pink with feathery swirls, a paisley print in reds and purples . . .

She chose a long-sleeved white blouse with eyelet trim and a soft, dark blue skirt with simple lines. After she had washed her hair and blown it dry, she had to admit she did look nice.

The look in Joel's eyes told her she did, too. And Tam was quick to pick up on it. "You look nice dressed up, Micky," she said approvingly.

"You do too," Micky said quickly, noting Tam's straight tan denim skirt.

Joel looked decidedly out of character in gray dress pants, a dark green cotton knit sweater with a V-neck, and white shirt. His red-brown hair looked curlier than ever.

"I'm so glad you could come," he said as he backed the car around and headed up the hill.

Micky chose to ignore Tam's giggle. "It was nice of you to pick me up," she said sedately.

"How has your week been?" Joel asked.

"Never a dull moment," Micky said. "Let's see. . . . Yesterday I visited Jim over at the hatchery. The day before that I practiced casting down by the open space where Loretta has her little trees growing.

"And I've read a lot." She didn't say *where* she'd read. Those hours she'd spent perched on the limb outside the window were somehow special—private. It had been a different world tucked high above the ground, enclosed in the tree's white-scented arms.

A feeling of sadness swept through her. The blossoms were almost gone, drifting away in the lazy warm days following the rain.

Church that morning was a jumbled confusion of strange faces, unfamiliar surroundings. But she liked Mr. Hoffman, the Sunday school teacher.

He made her feel comfortable right away with his friendly, "You came with the Brentwoods? So glad you did!"

She listened intently to his words. He was teaching from the vision of the prophet Isaiah. He made it come alive: the prostrate prophet, the flaming coal, a God of glory seated on His throne.

She looked across at Joel. He was listening with quiet concentration, a slight frown creasing his forehead. Mr. Hoffman's voice faded as she watched Joel; a shaft of sunlight through the window streaked through his reddish curls, highlighting them in gold.

He caught the intent of her gaze and turned toward her, flashing a smile. Micky flushed and lowered her eyes.

During the discussion that followed, her attention was captured. The class was so eager—so excited!

"I'm reading Isaiah, as you suggested, Mr. Hoffman," Joel said, "not so much to understand the vision as to see how Isaiah saw God."

Mr. Hoffman nodded. "Did you notice how many times Isaiah called God the Lord of hosts?"

"Yes," Joel said. "And chapter twenty-eight showed me even more about what God is like. I wrote, 'My Lord is': at the top of the paper, then listed every attribute I could find that described Him."

He flipped through the pages of his Bible and drew out a piece of paper. "My Lord is a crown of glory," he began, "a diadem of beauty, a tested stone, a precious cornerstone, a sure foundation, my teacher and instructor, the Lord of hosts, wonderful in counsel, excellent in working!" He lifted his head. "Isn't that awesome? And it's all in chapter twenty-eight!"

A small, slim girl leaned forward. " 'The Lord of hosts' caught my attention, too. I looked it up in my concordance and found a verse in Micah 4:4 that really impressed me: 'But they shall sit every man under his vine and under his fig tree; and none shall make them afraid; for the mouth of the Lord of hosts hath spoken it.' "

She lifted her head. "God's people had been taken away from their homes by this time and were living in strange lands. They wanted to be back in their own homes. And God, the mighty Lord of hosts, understood their heart's desires and promised each of them a place of their own."

Micky could identify, and a sudden yearning welled up within her.

The girl continued, "Understanding how much God loved them makes me realize how much He loves me and cares about me in the same way."

Afterward, in the foyer, Joel introduced Micky to

his parents. "Mom and Dad, this is Micky, our friend living with the Middletons."

"Nice to meet you, Micky." William Brentwood shook her hand warmly. "I'm Bill, and this is my wife, Eileen. We're happy you could come this morning with Joel and Tam. They tell us you enjoy the outdoors—the animals and Eagle Creek."

Micky could see Joel's kind eyes in his father's. And Joel's gentle smile was a copy of his mother's.

"Yes," Micky answered. "I do enjoy nature a lot. I'm sure Joel told you about our rescuing a young doe from the creek the other day."

"Yes, that was quite an adventure," Bill chuckled, "and I'm sure there will be more. Shall we go in and sit down for the service?"

––––––––

Joel, Micky, and Tam had barely settled themselves in the car when Tam turned eagerly to Micky. "Well, did you like it?"

"Yes, I did," Micky confessed. "Especially the Sunday school class. It almost made me want to go home and start reading Isaiah—and I don't think I could even find it in the Bible."

Tam nodded. "I felt that way last winter when we were studying the book of John. If you've never read the Bible much, Micky, that's a good place to start."

Joel started the car. "Yeah, I can see why Mr. Hoffman had us study John before Isaiah. It makes the majesty and sovereignty of God more meaningful when we realize that His Son walked on the earth."

––––––––

Micky mulled over Joel's words when she got

home. She found a Bible in an open-shelved bookcase beside the fireplace. When she pulled it out, she spotted a folded piece of yellowed paper behind the bookcase, between the baseboard and the wall. Almost without thinking she picked up a pencil and attempted to free the paper.

After several tries to draw it out, she finally had it. Unfolding the sheet, the words sprang up at her:

> If you really love me and can forgive me for not being the person you wanted me to be, you can find me at Paul Larson's house, 103 S. Aaron Rd., Spring Valley, California.
> Love,
> Jamie

Micky's first impulse was to show the note to Loretta. She jumped to her feet, then stood still.

The note was written nine years ago, she thought. How would reading it now help matters? How would it make Loretta feel?

"I'll write Jamie myself," Micky decided. "Maybe, just maybe . . ."

Slowly she refolded the note and tucked it into the Bible. "Poor Jamie; poor Kent and Loretta. I wonder if anyone ever found this note." The conviction grew within her that they had not. If they'd seen it they surely would not have replaced it where it was . . . unless it had fallen behind . . .

———————

That night Micky wrote two letters—one to the long-lost Jamie, another to the unknown Paul Larson of Spring Valley.

Afterward, she opened the Bible to the gospel of

John and began to read: "In the beginning was the Word and the Word was with God, and the Word was God. . . ."

————

The next week raced by. Loretta was planning a wedding shower for Lucille's daughter, and the house had to be perfectly clean and in order for the big evening.

Micky and Loretta vacuumed floors, washed windows, polished furniture, and scoured sinks. Loretta spent hours in the kitchen planning the games and preparing the punch and cake.

Micky stood admiring the finished product. The cake was beautiful, shaped like a bell, garnished with pink roses and tiny silver leaves.

Like May Day, Micky thought, *with flowers and all—sounds like fun*. Anticipation rushed through her.

Loretta smiled at her. "Micky, the punch bowl's stored in our closet. Would you mind getting it down for me and washing it?"

Micky nodded and hurried into Kent and Loretta's bedroom. She opened the closet door. The punch bowl, wrapped in clear plastic, was on the top shelf.

As she reached for it, the vase beside it started to topple. Micky gasped and tried to catch it. But she was too late. The vase hit the edge of a chair, shattering into a dozen pieces.

"Oh, no!" she cried.

Then Kent was standing in the doorway. Before she saw him Micky bent to pick up the fragments.

"What are you doing in here?" he demanded coldly. "That vase was my mother's! How could you be so careless?"

"I—I—" Micky stammered, "I didn't mean to, I—"

"Of course you didn't mean to but, the fact remains, you broke a very old and valuable vase!"

Micky looked up at him. She felt her throat tighten, her eyes blur. "I'm very sorry," she whispered. "I was just getting the punch bowl down for Loretta. It was an accident—"

Kent turned on his heels and left the room in a huff.

Micky swallowed hard. Through her tears she noticed Margot's picture on the dresser.

You would never do something like this, would you, Margot. You weren't clumsy like me. And he loved you— just the way you were!

Micky leaped to her feet, anger and bitterness filling her heart. What would it be like to be the much loved, protected daughter of the house? To really belong?

On impulse she turned Margot's picture to the wall, then ran out the door. She almost collided with Loretta. But Micky rushed past her through the living room and out the front door. Almost without thinking she turned toward the hatchery.

She'd look at the fish, the little ones. They wouldn't care that she wasn't Margot, that she didn't belong.

She leaned over the runway, peering into the water. There was a light step behind her. A hand dropped to her shoulder.

"I didn't mean to," Micky whispered. The tears, which had been threatening, started to fall. She put her face in her hands.

"What is it, Micky? What's hurt you?"

Startled, Micky looked up into Jim's dark blue eyes. She had expected Loretta. *Strange,* she thought, *his eyes are the same color as Kent's.* But Jim's showed compassion while Kent's were like an impenetrable wall.

"The vase," Micky whispered. "I broke a valuable vase. It belonged to Kent's mother."

Jim nodded, his eyes understanding. "That's bad," he agreed, "but hardly the end of the world."

"But you don't know him!" Micky blurted. "He's so . . . so unreasonable." Then she fell silent. There were no words to explain the mixed-up feelings that churned inside her.

"I know. It's hard when you never feel like your best is good enough—"

"Margot . . . she was everything to him . . ."

A startled look crossed Jim's face. "And you?"

"Me? I'm not anything to them right now. Not their daughter, not even their friend."

"But you are a very special person, Micky. You've got to believe that. People are far more important than things. He'll get over it. You wait and see."

Micky brushed the tears from her eyes. "Do you really think so?" she asked.

"Yes, I do, I really do."

His words were a comfort to Micky. "Why do you think he's always so angry?" she asked curiously .

Jim had a sad, wistful look again. "He's suffered a lot. Sometimes people don't know how to deal with their grief and they take out their frustrations on those closest to them."

A flush rose into Micky's cheeks. "Oh, I see. Maybe he doesn't really hate me, after all."

"No, I'm sure he doesn't, Micky. Give him some time. He'll come around." Jim gave her a gentle shove.

"Better get back up to the house now. Loretta will be worried about you."

"Yeah, I guess you're right. Thanks, Jim."

Loretta met her at the door.

"Micky!" she exclaimed. "I was worried about you. Kent told me what happened. It's okay. It was an accident. You are more valuable than any vase, believe me. You are like a daughter to us, Micky, really you are."

"But Kent—"

Loretta wrapped her arms around her. "He'll get over it. He overreacted, that's all. People are more important than things. He'd be the first to agree."

As Micky rested her head against Loretta's shoulder, she thought, *Strange. Jim said the very same thing.*

9

May Day and Mrs. Morton

*T*he morning of the long-awaited May Day celebration dawned clear.

Like a golden chick just hatched from its egg, Micky thought, as she brushed her hair to shining perfection. Butterflies fluttered in her stomach. "My school debut," she said aloud to the mirror.

Loretta turned as Micky entered the kitchen. "You look nice, Micky," she remarked. "It was worth all those hours we spent searching for just the right outfit." A teasing smile spread across her face. "How about fixing a fresh bouquet of flowers for the breakfast table?"

Micky nodded, her thoughts not really on tradition. She took the shears Loretta handed her and went outside. On the porch, she almost tripped over a delicate arrangement of snowy lily of the valley mingled with fern fronds and tucked inside a basket.

Micky gasped and stooped to pick up the fragile gift. As she buried her face in its soft fragrance, her nose brushed the edge of a tiny note tucked inside. She saw her name on it and drew it out, wondering who would send her flowers. Inside, the note said simply, "You're special."

Micky took a deep breath. Suddenly the old tradition of May baskets and flowers didn't seem so trite!

She hurried inside to show Loretta. "It's for me!" she cried. Then seeing the expression on Loretta's face she added, "You knew!"

Loretta laughed and hugged her. "Of course! I almost knocked it over when I opened the door." She smiled knowingly at Micky. "I thought May baskets went out years ago. Somebody must be reviving an old tradition."

"I don't know who they're from," Micky said wistfully, "but I think we all should enjoy them." She set the basket in the middle of the table and stepped back to admire the flowers' delicate beauty.

"What's all this about flowers on the doorstep?" Kent asked as he and Steve came into the kitchen. He winked at her playfully as he sat down.

Steve cocked his eyebrows. "Joel?"

Micky shook her head as she too sat down. "I don't know." She felt the pink rise to her cheeks, and she suddenly felt beautiful—really beautiful, the torment of feeling unloved far behind her. She slipped her fingers beneath her napkin and pinched her leg to be sure she was really awake.

———

May Day was everything Joel and Tam had said it would be and more: the flower-decked court, the queen, her attendants and their escorts, the marching bands, gymnastic tumblers. . . .

The girls' P.E. classes had combined and did a marching formation of figure eights and geometric designs. Micky searched for Tam's long legs and red hair among the group. She spotted her at last, her shoulders and legs moving rhythmically, not missing a beat.

The Maypole dance was next. Freshman girls in

long, floating pastel dresses, gracefully dipped and swayed, somehow managing to artfully weave the long streamers around each pole.

"I did that when I was a freshman," Tam said as she slid onto the bleacher seat beside Micky. "The relays and games are next." They watched as the boys moved the poles to the edge of the field. "Enjoying it?"

"Yes, I am!" Micky enthused. "And everyone is so friendly."

A hush fell over the crowd as a clown with a long, sad face climbed the steps to the flower-decked court. Micky giggled as he began to carefully dust the podium. His suit was bright red and yellow, and a purple polka-dotted cape was draped over his shoulders.

The attendants and their escorts drew back, laughing, as the clown proceeded to dust the girls' dresses with his large feather duster. Then waving his duster before the queen and bowing before her, he swept the cape from his shoulders and in one smooth motion, laid it at her feet.

As if on cue, she tossed her bouquet into the air, and the clown leaped up and caught it, twirling around in a circle of delight.

The band struck up a lively tune, and the clown led the royal court in a majestic dance. Then girls with pom-pons spread out in a line before the spectators, and motioned everyone to join them on the field for the grand finale. It was easy to follow the simple steps, and the field vibrated with color and movement.

"Until the clown appeared on the scene, I thought the Maypole was best," Micky commented as she rode home with Joel and Tam.

Joel had an amused look on his face, and Tam threw back her head and laughed.

"What's so funny?" Micky asked, puzzled.

"It's just that . . . Should I tell her, Joel?"

"I was the clown," Joel said, stifling a laugh.

"No one at school guessed who it was!" Tam exclaimed. "It's unbelievable!"

Micky turned and stared at Joel. "You know, I did think the clown was somehow familiar, but . . ." Her cheeks flushed. "You did an awfully good job, Joel. Have you done it before?"

Joel smiled at her. "Yeah. I started last summer, helping with the Vacation Bible School at church. The kids loved it."

Tam bounced between them. "I even filled in for him one day, and they never guessed. It's something we can both do." She made a face at her brother. "But he works harder at it, I must admit."

After they'd let Tam out at a friend's house, Joel and Micky rode in silence. *What an unusual mixture of talents he has,* Micky thought. *Tam says he plays football—that he's one of the school's top players. And he fishes. Now this. I wonder if he'd be any good at finding missing persons?*

"What are you thinking?" Joel asked.

"Oh, nothing. Except . . . Joel, you seem to be involved in a lot of things."

"Yeah, I guess so," he said. "Is something bothering you?"

"Well, actually, I've been thinking about the Middletons' missing son," she said slowly. "It started when I moved into his former room and found a totem pole that he'd carved. There was a letter inside it, and then last week, I found a note he'd written. . . . That would be nine years ago, though."

Quickly she recounted how she'd written a couple of letters to try to locate him.

"Aside from the letters, I don't think there's much you can do, Micky," Joel said when she'd finished. "Nine years is a long time."

Micky nodded. "You're right, but I wish I could do more—for his brother Steve's sake. He always seems to be struggling, never measuring up to his father's expectations."

They pulled into the driveway and Micky started to get out, but Joel put a hand on her shoulder.

"I have something for you." He reached into the backseat, and then gently laid the queen's bouquet on her lap.

"Oh!" Micky cried. "It's beautiful!" She inhaled the perfume of the delicate rosebuds, white carnations, and dainty baby's breath. "I don't know what to say!"

Joel just smiled, and Micky saw a tenderness in his face that she'd not seen before. As she turned again to leave, she saw a familiar car in the driveway. "It's Mrs. Morton," she said, "my caseworker. Goodbye, Joel. And thank you—for a wonderful day."

She watched as Joel backed his green Chevrolet out, then stepped up to greet Mrs. Morton who was just getting out of her car.

Micky held the flowers out. "Aren't they beautiful!"

Mrs. Morton seemed to ignore them, her thoughts obviously on other things. "I don't know how to tell you this, Micky, but . . . I have some news for you. Let's go inside."

Loretta met them at the door. She started to exclaim over the bouquet, until she saw Mrs. Morton's expression. "There's a vase under the sink for your flowers, Micky."

Loretta and Mrs. Morton went into the living room, and Micky filled a wide green vase with water. She could barely hear the voices in the other room.

"I don't know how to tell her about her mother," she thought she heard Mrs. Morton say.

Micky turned off the water and rushed into the living room, "What is it?" Micky cried. "Please, tell me."

Loretta put both arms around her. "Sit down, Micky," she said. "It's all right, just unexpected."

Micky looked intently at Loretta's face, trying to detect what was wrong. She thought her eyes looked on the verge of tears.

Mrs. Morton came directly to the point. "We've found your mother, Micky," she said. "Actually, she found us."

"But . . . but—" Micky cried.

"She's very ill. She had a nurse call our office. She'd like to see you."

Micky licked her lips. "Where is she?"

"At a hospital in Portland. She's registered as Joanne Cochran." Mrs. Morton stood up. "Whether or not you wish to see her is entirely up to you, Micky. If you want to go I'll take you. If not," She spread her hands in a helpless gesture. "I'll send her word."

Micky walked to the window. The delicate green veil that had seemed to float over the alders and vine maples was deeper now. The tender new leaves moved in the quiet breeze. Beyond, the creek flashed its presence.

Mother's eyes were like the stream, Micky thought. *Why did she leave me? How could she do it?*

Loretta came over and stood beside her. "If you want to see her, I'll go with you."

Micky shook her head. "No. If I go, I'll go alone."

She wasn't sure if she wanted to. *She left me when I needed her. What right does she have to come back into my life now? Just when I'm beginning to be happy again.*

Abruptly she turned to Loretta. "What do you think I should do?" she asked.

Loretta took a deep breath. "You're old enough to make your own decision, Micky, but I can tell you this, if you refuse to see her, it may be something you'll regret the rest of your life. She *is* your mother."

"I'll go then," Micky said matter-of-factly. She broke away from Loretta's steadying arm.

"Better take a sweater, Micky," Mrs. Morton suggested. "It's getting cool."

Micky nodded. Upstairs she pulled a white cardigan off a hanger, then stepped to the window and leaned out. *Peaceful days—wonderful days—now this.*

She took a deep breath and clattered down the stairs. "I've decided not to go," she said. "Maybe later—maybe never."

Without another word she turned and left the room. The dark fir trees at the edge of the garden beckoned to her. She went deep into the woods.

It was a while before she noticed the firs murmuring in the wind, a chattering squirrel, a dove cooing in the distance. Then a blue jay began to call, flashing from limb to limb.

Micky found a stump in a clearing and sat down. A deer stopped at the edge of the vine maple-trimmed meadow and looked at her. Micky drew in her breath. The doe flicked its white tail and bounded away.

Morning—could it have been Morning?

Then Micky fell into a daydream. A tiny elf, not much bigger than a drop of water, clambered onto a tiny mushroom. Another swung from a moss-draped limb. They were calling to Morning, telling her that Micky wouldn't hurt her, that she cared.

Micky stood and walked deeper into the woods. Here the tightly interwoven branches overhead formed a canopy. She could picture it in winter, the topside of the canopy lashed by fierce wind and rain, while beneath, the ferns and bushes would scarcely move.

Vaguely, she wondered what lived up there. Most of the birds she had observed seemed to be building their nests in the thickets or even on the ground. An unseen creature scuttled beneath a clump of hazel-brush—going home.

All of a sudden Micky knew what she must do.

10

Mother

"*I*'ve decided I need to see my mother after all." Micky stood in the kitchen, her hair tangled and dirt on her shoes.

Loretta turned from the counter where she was cutting biscuits. A slight frown creased her forehead, but her eyes said she was pleased.

"I'm glad," she said quietly.

Micky pulled a rosebud and a tangled bit of baby's breath from the vase she'd left on the counter. "I could take these—"

"That would be nice." Loretta wiped her fingers on a paper towel and put her hand on Micky's shoulder. "You've made a difficult decision, Micky, and I'm proud of you." She moved away. "I'll drive you in after dinner."

The long ride into Portland was a haze in Micky's mind. Her fingers clutched her rose as she dully observed the maze of bridges, the lights reflecting off the Willamette River . . .

Loretta left her at the curb of the busy hospital, promising to meet her later in the waiting room after she'd found a parking place.

Micky spoke briefly to a busy woman behind a desk. The elevator took her upstairs, then she proceeded down the long hallway. She walked past nurses; peered at the numbers over bustling wards; caught glimpses of white-gowned patients, some in beds, others wandering the halls.

A man with tubes protruding everywhere had been left on a stretcher outside a crowded ward—asleep—but alone. Micky's throat suddenly ached. Her eyes burned. She hurried quickly away.

Finally, number 337 stood out to her over a door and she stopped. A salty taste filled her mouth; cold sweat broke out on the palms of her hands. She had to force herself not to hold her stomach, which had become weak and churning.

She stepped through the door, her chin up. "Mother—"

A dark-haired woman in the bed was looking out the window and turned toward her. She held out her hand uncertainly. "Michelle?"

Micky stepped closer. "Yes, it's me. I heard you wanted to see me."

They looked at each other—a long, searching look that failed to span the years they'd been apart.

The woman nervously ran a hand through her short-cropped hair.

"I-I'm glad you came. I—"

"I didn't know where you were," Micky explained. "You never wrote—or called—"

The long, thin hands gripped the edge of the blanket. "I was here—here in Portland."

"I-I tried to find you when I was little," Micky whispered. "How could you leave me? And my brothers—Kevin, Alan—where are they?"

The woman's eyes shifted around the room. "Haven't heard much from Kevin," she muttered. "He never writes."

"And Alan?"

The haunted eyes returned to Micky's face. "He didn't turn out so good," she said. "He's in a special school—here in town." She twisted the edge of the sheet around her fingers. "I'm not a good woman," she whispered, "but I did love you."

"I tried to find you," Micky repeated, "and all the time you were here in Portland." It was a statement, not a question.

"I used my maiden name," she explained. She leaned back on her pillow. "You never knew, Michelle, but the boys weren't really Strands. I don't even know who their fathers are.

"That's why I left you. I didn't deserve you. Your real father did."

"But he left me, too!" Micky cried. "And before he did, we just went from place to place." A vision of sagging porches, ancient gas stoves, and hooks to hang up her clothes flashed before her. A bitter taste filled her mouth. "Then one day he was gone . . ."

She fell silent. It had started then, the round of foster homes. She saw herself, a plain, sullen girl, not quite belonging in any of them.

"When I was twelve they told me my father had died." The silence deepened. She remembered that she'd cried a little that night, not because of all the unhappiness he'd led her through, but because she didn't understand. She had known he loved her in his simple, inadequate way. Like the day he'd put his arms around her when she'd run away from her fourth-grade class, the Christmas morning she'd found the big white teddy bear at the foot of her bed. . . .

Her mother's hand reached out and touched hers. "I'm sorry," she whispered, "but you're my baby girl. Can't you forgive me—love me—a little?"

Micky suddenly fell to her knees beside the bed, covering her face in the bedspread. "I don't know!" she cried. "A tiny piece inside me says I do love you. But I just don't know!" She lifted her head. "I never let anyone call me Michelle because you were the only one who ever did—back then. I thought it was your own special name for me.

"But I can't understand why you would leave me. Just because the boys weren't Daddy's—"

"I had to get away," the woman whispered. "I couldn't stand those four walls, no money. And before that, the shouting . . ."

Get away . . . The words stirred inside Micky. She leaped to her feet and looked down at her mother. "I have to go now . . ." She tried to say "Mother," but the word stuck in her throat.

The woman clutched at Micky's hands. Suddenly Micky remembered her rose. "Here," she said, thrusting it toward her mother.

Then Micky was running—out the door, down the hall. She almost collided with Loretta, who was hurrying toward her, an anxious look on her face. "Micky—"

"I've seen her already!" Micky exclaimed. "Let's go—"

The evening air cooled her burning cheeks. She took a deep breath, then turned to Loretta. "She's sick—really sick. I can see that. But Loretta, it was so awful!"

Loretta grabbed her arm and hurried alongside her. "We're parked over here."

Once inside the car Micky buried her face in her hands and burst into tears. "I'm not crying just because she's sick," she wailed, "but because everything is so different from what I imagined meeting my mother would be. I had such dreams. All she wanted was for me to forgive her because she left me, and I-I found out I couldn't!"

Loretta's hand groped for hers. "It's all right, Micky. Everything will be all right."

But it wasn't. All night Micky tossed and turned. A tangled web of feeling kept tugging inside her; resentment, pity, then pain.

"She should never have asked me to come," she whispered into the darkness. "She had no right to ask me." Then later, "But she is my mother. I should love her. But I don't."

As dawn interrupted the darkness, she lay in bed and watched the sunlight gradually lighten the wide-winged eagle, the tiny deer, the queen's bouquet she'd placed on her dressing table. *Joel,* she thought, *dear Joel*.

After breakfast, Micky slipped away to the fish hatchery. Perhaps if she could talk to Jim, he would understand.

He took one look at her as she stood in the doorway. He put down the tray he was carrying and came over to her. "What's up, Micky?"

Slowly, haltingly, Micky began. She told him first of the wonderful May Day morning, then about the message her caseworker brought, and the awfulness of facing the woman who'd left her so many years ago. Together Micky and Jim left the building, walking past the runways and the holding tank. They stopped at the bridge and leaned over the railing, neither one seeing the dashing, laughing creek beneath them.

"I don't see why it had to happen now—why it had to be so different than I'd dreamed."

A question formed in Jim's eyes.

"Sometimes I'd imagine that she'd come searching for me," Micky admitted, "that we'd see each other and all the pain would be magically forgotten. Other times I'd pretend I was meeting her and quietly tell her what an awful woman she was for failing me and my father. I'd shout at her that she had no right to run off with my brothers—

"But lately, I've been thinking less about her. Somehow I was beginning to want to get on with my own life. Then, there she was. When I saw her, she wasn't at all like I'd imagined she'd be. I hardly recognized her; her hair was short, and she didn't seem the same at all."

Micky propped her elbows on the railing and held her face between her hands. "I think what bothers me most now is that I see something of myself in her, the part I don't like—always running from what's painful or hard. And yet sometimes, I just long to go back—to that little yellow house."

She lifted her face. "Did you ever have a place like that, Jim? A place that was sheltered and happy?"

Jim nodded slowly. "Mine was high up in a treetop. I felt so secure and happy up there—"

"Mine was underneath a snowball bush. My brothers and I would crawl inside and be in a world apart, our own little world. Nothing could hurt us there, not our mother, not our father.

"Sometimes Mother would call me and I'd pretend I didn't hear her. Then she'd call again, 'Michelle! Michelle Ann Strand!' "

Jim looked at her, light dawning in his dark blue eyes. "Is that why you wanted to be called Micky?"

"I-I . . . Yes, I guess that's why."

Jim put an arm around her shoulders. "Michelle," he said softly. "It's a lovely name."

"But a name that hurts," Micky cried. Her chin trembled. "Whenever someone calls me Michelle, I remember the rejection, the pain. Do you think it will ever go away?"

Jim's hand tightened on Micky's shoulder, and she looked at him. His eyes searched the water, but Micky knew he saw something beyond it.

"I don't have the answer to that one, Micky," he said at last. "Will the past always follow us and haunt us if we keep running from it?"

His arm dropped from her shoulders, and he turned from her. Micky watched him—a lonely man, the weight of his thoughts bending his shoulders as he walked away, leaving her there.

A sharp pain gripped her heart. "Oh, Jim," she murmured, "could it be that you are running away from something too?"

11

Away! Away!

"Who do you know in Spring Valley?" Kent asked, dropping a letter beside Micky's plate.

A hot flush colored Micky's cheeks as she picked it up. Kent, Loretta, and Steve looked at her expectantly.

"No one, really. Just a friend of a friend—sort of." She slid the letter into her shirt pocket and smiled at them.

"I've been reading Steve's *Audubon* magazines," she said, eager to change the subject. "Did you know that no two robins sing exactly the same way?"

"What do you mean?" Steve asked, his blue eyes flashing interest.

"Each robin varies its song, puts phrases together differently. Even an individual robin will sing as many as ten different songs, depending somewhat on the time of day."

Loretta laid down her fork. "I never knew that. It's fascinating, isn't it?"

Micky nodded. "I think it's true, too. When I wake up early, it seems I can identify different robin tunes. And one night I was sure I heard a robin sing in the rain. It was so sad, and yet so beautiful."

"Don't you sleep well, Micky?" Kent asked.

Micky shrugged. "Oh, yes, but sometimes I wake

up real early, and occasionally in the middle of the night."

It was true. She sometimes felt restless in her new home. It wasn't easy to adjust to another family. So when she'd awake early in the morning, she'd simply lie in bed and listen to the birds' riotous chorus.

Sometimes she got up and wandered among Loretta's roses. June had come in all its splendor, with great pink blooms as large as saucers, lovely peace roses, and the scarlet and gold piccadilly. Their petals gleamed with dew, fragrant with distilled sweetness.

After dinner, Micky offered to help clean up, even though the letter begged her to find her own secret place. Loretta jostled her good-naturedly.

"Not tonight. Go read your letter before it burns a hole in your pocket."

Gratefully, Micky hurried up the stairs. Her open window welcomed the good, outdoor smell of growing things. Micky climbed out, stepping onto the limb that led her to the tree's heart.

From long practice, she snuggled her back against the perfectly shaped seat and pulled out her letter.

Dear Micky,

Thank you for your letter and your interest in my friend Jamie. Jamie stayed with me several years. He has since moved, and I've lost track of him. However, I did forward your letter to his last address.

Disappointment, coupled with a wild elation, rose inside Micky. If only Jamie himself had written; but at least he was alive. Perhaps he would get in touch with her—someday.

I'll write him again, she decided. *Surely his friend will forward it.*

It was good to have something exciting to think about; her days had been stretching endlessly, making her almost wish she were back in school. Joel and Tam were rushed with end-of-the-year activities. They still picked her up on Sundays, but Micky longed for something more. Every time she brushed one of Loretta's rosebuds against her nose, her thoughts drifted back to the queen's bouquet.

She still kept it on her dresser. Every morning the dried roses and baby's breath tickled her nose. Every night it was the last thing she looked at when she turned off the light.

Micky stuck the letter in her pocket and climbed back inside her room. She went downstairs and into the garden where she snipped a long-stemmed rose and selected a fern frond from the clump growing by the back door. Back inside, she arranged them in a slender white vase, then stepped back to admire the arrangement.

Kent and Loretta's voices came in through the open doorway.

"It isn't right, Kent!" Loretta argued. "He doesn't want to go. Not deep inside."

"You're making him into a weakling!" Kent declared. "He needs to do the things he's afraid of!"

"But in his own time, Kent. On his own!"

"It's just a silly fear he has, Loretta."

Loretta's voice was shrill. "Here you go again," she cried, "always pushing, pushing, never content with who or what your sons are!"

"Just a minute, Loretta!"

"You pushed Jamie away with your foolish expectations. Now you're doing it to Steve! He's afraid of heights. Afraid! And you're forcing him to go rock rappelling, because—because you think it will make a man of him!"

There was a sudden silence. Micky swallowed hard and made herself walk into the living room. A door slammed. Kent was gone.

Loretta sat alone on the couch, staring into space. She didn't even look up.

Micky went over and timidly touched her shoulder.

"He's taking Steve rock rappelling at Smith Rock tomorrow," Loretta said dully. "I don't want them to go."

"It's good for fathers and sons to go off together sometimes," Micky ventured.

"I-I know. But Steve's terribly afraid of heights."

"Perhaps if he faced up to it. You told me once I shouldn't always run away from what I fear."

Loretta smiled, an empty smile that didn't come from her heart. She sighed audibly. "But this is different—a phobia over which he has no control."

Micky looked down at the rose still clutched in her hand. She held it out. "It's for you, Loretta."

Loretta took the white vase. "Oh, it's lovely. You have a flair for things like this." She stood up. "Thank you, dear. And don't fret about Kent and Steve. They'll be fine."

She left the room, and Micky went in search of Steve. She found him in the basement curled up with a book.

"Hi!" she said brightly. "Care if I join you?"

Steve's blue gaze was clouded with gray and was anything but welcoming. "Suit yourself," he grunted. He turned a page and went on reading.

"I hear you're going rock rappelling in the morning. Where at?"

"Smith Rock."

"Where's that?"

"Prineville area."

"Excited?"

Steve put his book down and glared at her. "You don't have to stay down here," he said coldly.

Micky was undaunted. "I want to," she said. "I'm tired of being alone all day, and I need someone to talk to."

"Go talk to the robins."

"I already have. I need a person."

"Well," he said with exaggerated courtesy, "what shall we talk about?"

"Rock rappelling. Are you afraid, Steve?"

Steve moved his taut shoulders restlessly. "Of course not."

Micky cocked her head to one side. "But I think you are."

She now had his complete attention. His eyes seemed more gray than blue as they bore into hers. "What makes you think so?"

"I heard your mom say you were afraid of heights. Have you always been?"

Steve took a deep breath. "Ever since I can remember, they've bothered me. Even going over some bridges makes me feel nervous inside. And you've never seen Smith Rock. It goes almost straight up."

"Why does your dad want you to do this?"

"Because he's afraid!" he said scornfully.

"Your dad?"

"He's afraid I'll turn out like Jamie. Run off, never amount to anything." He turned his face away. "And

I'm afraid too, afraid he'll never ever think I'm anybody worthwhile."

He jumped to his feet. "I'm climbing that rock, Micky. I have to . . ."

I'm climbing that rock. I have to. I have to, echoed in Micky's thoughts. *In a way he's running away, too,* she realized. *Away from the person he was meant to be.*

She went up the stairs, through the living room, and on up to her own room. Her Bible lay beside her bed.

She slipped to her knees. "I wish I knew how to pray," she whispered.

———

That night Micky dreamed. A huge rock as big as a house teetered on a bluff. Her two brothers, just as she remembered them, played contentedly at its base.

A great fear overwhelmed her as the rock started to move. She must get to them!

"Micky! Micky!" Kevin screamed. There was a crash, then total blackness. Micky jerked up in bed, her heart pounding.

"Kevin," she whispered. "Oh, Kevin. Are you all right?"

The darkness mocked her. She turned on the light and peered at the clock—five minutes past twelve. The urgency of the dream haunted her. She pulled on her robe and crept down the stairs.

Kent sat alone in the living room, the TV turned low. He held up his hand, silencing her, intent on hearing every word.

Feeling even more alone, Micky slipped into the kitchen. Perhaps a cup of hot chocolate would send the dream from her mind.

She shivered as she waited for the water to boil, then turned. Kent stood in the doorway, scowling.

"What are you doing up?" he demanded. "Aren't you happy here either?"

"Why . . . I-I just couldn't sleep. I had a dream. There was a rock. It was falling—"

"You too?" he roared. "Is everyone in this family against me?"

Micky stared at him, unable to comprehend what he meant. "You mean Steve?" she blurted.

"You're two of a kind!" he stated angrily. "You're both afraid of your own shadows. Only with you, it's your past. You've let it bind you all up. And where does it get you? Nowhere!"

Micky opened her mouth to speak, but no words came. She ran past him, up the stairs, and into her room. Tears of frustration burned her eyes.

She tossed her robe onto the pillow and began to pull on her jeans, warm socks, and a hooded sweatshirt. Then she slipped out the window and down the tree. She jumped to the ground and ran.

Jim, if she could just talk to Jim. He'd been her special friend since the day she'd confided to him about her mother. Kent and Loretta had said she should go back to see her, but Jim never did. Somehow she felt he understood the turmoil that raged inside her.

She stood outside his door, knocking nervously. There was no answer. She tapped lightly on the window. Still no response.

After a while she plodded back to the road, starting off slowly, then picking up the pace—away from Kent, Loretta, Steve, Jim. Once her breath caught on something that sounded like a sob, but she kept on, refusing to let the dam break.

She stopped at the top of the hill, where Loretta had picked her up before, and rested for a bit in the small shelter where the children waited for the school bus. She singled out the big dipper, low over a distant farmhouse. Somehow, it offered a small comfort.

Then she resumed her hike, her fingers jingling the change she'd stuffed into her pockets at the last minute. Slowly the night sky wheeled above her. But on she walked.

Toward morning, weariness overtook her, and she crept into a barn beside the road. She spread some hay beside the cows' stalls and lay down in the prickly nest.

"Jesus slept in a barn His first night on earth," she mused. Feeling comforted at the thought, she fell asleep.

She wakened with a large black-and-white dog barking over her. Quickly she sat up, putting out a friendly hand. "Here, doggie, nice doggie, shhh, doggie."

The dog stopped barking and stood still, wagging his tail ever so slightly. Then he lapped at her face with his wet tongue.

"No, doggie, no, no!"

Slowly she got to her feet. Her fingers felt like ice, and she thought longingly of the hot chocolate she'd never made before she left.

"Maybe I'll go to Spring Valley in California," she said to her ardent admirer. "Paul Larson took Jamie in. Maybe he'd take me, too." She stopped. Deep inside she knew she really wanted to go back to the Middletons.

"Kent's always yelling at someone. Well, not all the time, but—he's really a very miserable man.

"My mother said she couldn't stand to hear yelling

either. But I hate to think that I'm just like her. What do you think, doggie?"

The dog's entire body began to accompany his vigorously wagging tail. A smile broke the troubled look on Micky's face. She threw both arms around his great shaggy neck. "Oh, doggie," she whispered.

After a while she started down the road again. It was hard to convince the dog not to follow. "Home!" Micky commanded. "Home! Home!" He hesitated, but then started after her again, and Micky picked up some loose stones from the side of the road and threw them at the dog until he retreated and returned to the barn, his tail between his legs.

Tears started again as Micky thought, *Will I always hurt those who care for me?*

The sun rose high as she walked on, and cars were beginning to appear on the road. Several times she took shortcuts through the sparse woods and fields.

One of them was a strawberry field. Micky bent down and pushed the leaves back. A gleaming red strawberry, wet with dew, rewarded her.

"Mmmm," she sighed, popping it into her mouth. She searched for more, and after eating her fill she continued on her way.

Estacada was farther than she realized. The road seemed endless, each curve hiding a longer stretch than she'd remembered. Her thighs began to tremble and she had to stop and rest.

Even the town she'd once considered small seemed big now. She plodded down the streets until she saw a bus stop sign.

A woman passing by paused to speak to her. "Bus service on Sunday is poor," she said. "It will be at least an hour before one shows up."

Micky thanked her as she moved away. *Now what?* Her stomach growled, making her keenly aware of her hunger. Never had a cup of hot chocolate sounded more tempting. Those lovely strawberries she'd eaten seemed like a dream.

She began searching for some kind of cafe or restaurant. A small white building with a red and blue sign said: AL'S COUNTRY COOKING, and she stopped.

She fingered her coins as she moved closer and peered through the large window. A familiar head of reddish brown curly hair caught her eye. *Could it be Joel?*

Her heart clumped hard as her hand gripped the doorknob. *Should I go up to him or pretend not to see him?*

She stepped in to the noisy clatter of plates and silverware. The fragrance of coffee and frying bacon welcomed her.

Making a quick decision, Micky slid into the chair beside Joel. He looked at her, no surprise registering on his face. He beckoned the waitress. "Bring her some hash browns, bacon and eggs, and coffee."

The waitress slid a steaming cup in front of her.

"I don't like coffee," Micky whispered.

"Hot chocolate then," Joel said, "and add plenty of whipped cream."

"I already had breakfast," Micky protested feebly. "That is, I ate some strawberries in a field, and I would have had milk with them if I could have figured out how to get it out of the cow."

A smile broke the serious look on Joel's face. "Well," he countered, "I think we can do better than that."

Micky's throat thickened suddenly. "Why are you here? I would have thought you'd be in church."

Joel shook his head. "Not today. Loretta called me at three a.m., terrified. She asked if I had any idea where you might be."

"Oh, no!" Micky whispered, "I'm sorry."

"Then Kent took the phone. He sounded beside himself with worry. 'We've got to find her,' he said. So I got dressed, and I've been searching ever since." He made a sweeping gesture. "This was my last idea of where you might show up."

The waitress brought her hot chocolate, and Micky sipped it slowly, its warmth soothing her fears and taking the chill from her fingers.

"Did they think I was running away again?" she asked.

Joel nodded. "I've never heard them sound so worried. They really love you, Micky. Did you really mean to just walk out of their lives?"

"I-I don't know. I had this terrible dream. When I told Kent about it, he thought I was accusing him of something." She shook her head.

Joel touched her arm. "What's really bothering you, Micky? Haven't you been happy with the Middletons?"

"Sometimes," she whispered. "But I have this terrible longing, this yearning for—a place to call home. But I can never seem to find it."

The waitress brought their plates. "Oh," Micky murmured. "I've never been so hungry."

Joel took her hand, then bowed his head. "Thank you, Lord, for bringing Micky here. And thank you for this food." He squeezed her hand quickly and released it.

A flush rose in her cheeks, and she took a bite of the hash browns. "They're perfect, Joel. Thank you."

"Did you read the book of John, Micky?" he asked after a few moments.

She nodded. "Yes, I did. Then I started the book of Luke."

"Good. I read something in Matthew yesterday that made me think of you."

Micky stopped, her fork in hand. "Me?"

"Uh-huh. A man wanted to follow Jesus, but Jesus told him, 'Foxes have holes, and the birds of the air have nests, but the Son of Man has no where to lay His head.' "

"Jesus said that about himself?"

Joel nodded. "He didn't have a place to call home either, Micky, not after He was grown."

"Wow! Maybe He understands how I feel sometimes."

"He does understand, Micky. Trust me. And very few understood Him."

"But He had God, didn't He?" Micky protested.

Joel nodded. "Yes, of course. And so do we."

Micky leaped to her feet, sudden concern on her face. "I have to call Loretta, at least tell her where I am."

"Good idea. The telephone is in the back."

When Micky returned, her face shone. "I talked to all of them!" she exclaimed. "Loretta said Kent had just come in to see if she'd heard anything when the phone rang. He's coming to get me right away—Loretta too!"

"Steve?"

"He said he was glad I was coming back. Then he said something kind of funny before he hung up." Bewilderment clouded her eyes. "He said, 'Thanks, big sister.' "

———

It was only after she was safe at home, alone in her own room, that she understood Steve's words. Her running off had kept Kent and Steve from ascending Smith Rock!

She ran her fingers over the soaring eagle poised on top of the totem pole. "Well, old eagle friend, you can soar over rocks, but Steve can't. And you have a nest, too." She looked at her pillow. "And I have a place to put my head. . . . But Jesus . . ."

12

Peter Rabbit Remembers

*M*icky lay in bed, the darkness pressing around her. "Jesus, the Son of God, the Creator of the universe, with no place to lay His head . . ."

What would it be like to sleep on the ground? she wondered. She turned restlessly. What was it Joel had said right before Kent had come for her?

"There's something else about Jesus, Micky. Even though He didn't have a place to lay His head, He said that anyone who comes to Him will find a place in His heart, and He in theirs."

A great longing filled her. She wanted to find that place.

She slipped out of bed and padded to the window. The cherry leaves rustled invitingly, giving her glimpses of winking stars. The moonlight, shattered by leaves, flooded the lawn.

Micky went back to her bed and picked up the Indian blanket. Quietly, she stole down the stairs.

The ground beneath the cherry tree was hard and lumpy. She thought about going back for her pillow, then decided against it.

She tilted her head back and let the majesty of the stars fill her. With them came a sense of wonder: The Creator of those great blinking spheres came to earth as a tiny baby; His first bed was a manger filled with prickly hay.

Suddenly tears filled her eyes. "Jesus," she said, "the Sunday school teacher, Mr. Hoffman, says you're real, that I can talk to you. I'm not a good person, Jesus. I need you to forgive me, to take me to your heart, to live in mine."

Micky felt like she was beginning a new life. She could sleep in peace. The hard ground cradled her, and the Creator of the universe put His great loving arms around her and gathered His new child close to His heart.

———

Micky wakened suddenly. The dew on the grass was wet on her fingertips. For a moment she couldn't remember where she was. Then she turned her head and saw Kent's big boots pressing into the grass beside her. She looked up. A worried frown creased his forehead.

"You scared me to death, Micky," he said, his voice fraught with concern. "I thought you'd run off again."

Micky struggled to a sitting position, the blanket wrapped tightly around her. It felt a little odd, almost like a cocoon.

The sun wasn't up yet, the pink streamers hung over the tops of the trees. Birdsong filled the air.

She brushed her dark hair out of her eyes and smiled at Kent. "I'm sorry," she said. "I didn't mean to frighten you."

Kent squatted beside her. "What made you come out here?" he asked.

Micky squinted thoughtfully. "I kept thinking about God—His greatness and majesty. And then how

He left heaven and came to earth, and there was no place for Him here. It made me want to come out and look at the stars."

Kent was silent, his dark blue eyes fixed on the distant trees, the roaring creek. At last he spoke. "You think deep thoughts, Micky. You're a good kid." He stood up. "What would you like for breakfast, Micky girl?"

Micky grinned. "French toast," she said, "and I'm going to fix it!"

She leaped to her feet, still swathed in her blanket. They raced together for the door.

———

After breakfast, Micky sat for a long time in the living room. Both Kent and Loretta had gone off to work, and Steve to school. The day stretched long and unbroken before her.

A great longing rose inside her. She wanted to tell Joel and Tam about her decision out under the stars. Instead, she went upstairs, drawing her letter from Paul Larson out of the totem pole where she'd hidden it.

That afternoon she wrote a long letter to Jamie and put it into the mailbox. Perhaps if he knew that God was a God of new beginnings . . .

When she came in, she telephoned Tam. Tam answered right away, her voice eager.

"Ah," she teased, "Micky, the gal who comes to church just so she can date my good-looking brother. . . . Micky, are you there?"

Slowly Micky put down the receiver. "I can't tell her about last night," she whispered. "She'll think I did it to get Joel."

Another thought, even more terrible, raced through

her mind: *Joel will think that, too.*

She turned and ran from the room, the telephone shrilling behind her. She flew across the lawn, past the bridge, then climbed high up on the bluff overlooking the stream and hatchery.

She saw Jim's head silhouetted dark against the concrete background.

After a while she joined him beside the runway that held the smaller fish. He smiled at her, his nose twitching in the way she'd come to love. "Troubled again, Micky?"

Micky nodded. She sat down on the ledge and stared at him. "Jim, do you have many friends?"

Jim's nose twitched again. He raised his eyebrows into a question as he sat down beside her. *Just like Peter Rabbit,* she thought.

"Why do you ask, Micky?"

"Because today I tried to share something special with a friend. But she—"

"Misunderstood?"

"Not really. I didn't get a chance to tell her. She made a remark that made me hesitate, and then I just hung up."

"You can tell me, Micky, that is, if you want to."

"Yes, I do. You know how alone I've always felt, so out of things somehow?"

Jim nodded. "No place to call home."

"Right. Well, I've discovered something new." Micky struggled for words. "Joel told me about . . . about a person—Jesus Christ," she blurted.

"I see. Go on."

"He didn't have any place on earth to lay His head. People misunderstood Him. But He came for us. He has a place for us in His heart. And He longs to live in ours. . . . You told me once that you had a special place a long time ago when you were a boy. . . ."

Jim's dark eyes grew dreamy, reminiscent. "It was just outside my bedroom window. I'd crawl out, and there I'd be, looking down, way down. I could see the water flashing, the top of the grape arbor, the baby birches. Sometimes my mother would be out in the garden, kneeling among the carrots and tomatoes, her dark hair so smooth and shining. My baby brother toddling beside her—"

Micky took in a sharp breath. She stared at him. He frowned at her, the faraway look gone from his eyes. "Why are you looking at me like that?"

"Oh, it's nothing," she mumbled.

"Now—what were you saying before I went off on my childhood tangent?"

"Just that—that—Jesus is my special friend now. He's in my heart and I'm in His."

Jim stood up. He reached out and tousled her soft, dark hair. "I'm glad for you, Micky. Everyone needs a friend they can count on. Don't forget, I'm your friend too."

After he left, Micky sat there thinking. Tam's teasing words playing over and over in her mind.

Would everyone at church think she'd received Jesus just to get Joel? Micky pushed her troubled thoughts aside. Jim's reminiscences were more important right now.

———

After dinner, Micky climbed out her window and settled herself among the branches. She looked down and saw the flashing stream, the tops of the birch trees, Steve's brown hair.

Eagerly, she hurried down to join him. He was standing alone on the bank, watching the great gray fish lying at the bottom of the creek.

He smiled at her. "They're so beautiful, aren't they? I wonder what their world is like in the cold water?"

"Different than ours," Micky said, then changed the subject abruptly. "Did your family used to have grape arbors here? And a vegetable garden?"

"How did you know?" he asked curiously.

"I didn't . . . I just wondered."

Steve gestured toward the lawn. "We used to grow grapes there, along the edge. We took them out a few years ago because they weren't producing. And down in the low space, below where those tiny trees are growing—that used to be Mother's garden."

Micky nodded slowly. "Do you remember it much?"

"A little bit. Once I pulled out a whole bunch of carrots trying to help weed. I was real little then." He looked suddenly wistful. "I sort of miss it, in a way. But now that Mother works so much at the pharmacy, well, she can't do everything."

Micky agreed, then went in search of Loretta. She found her kneeling among her roses, a trowel in her hand, a can of rose food beside her. She leaned back on her heels and smiled at Micky.

"Do you have any old photo albums, Loretta? I'd like to see what everyone used to look like." She made a sweeping gesture. "And the house and the grounds."

Loretta got to her feet, wiping her hands on her stained blue jeans. She laid her trowel on the path and went inside.

Micky followed her into her bedroom. She seldom

went in there, but now she wanted an excuse to look at Margot's picture. Would there be a resemblance to Jim?

Loretta opened a drawer and pulled out several albums. Micky looked at Margot. Her dark brown eyes, her dimpling smile, all spoke of a much-loved, spoiled young girl. Micky frowned, but she could see no resemblance to Jim except for the shape of her large brown eyes.

"Did Jamie look like Margot?" she asked.

Loretta looked up. "Why, no—not especially. They were both dark though, nice looking with those big eyes. Only Jamie's were like his father's, dark blue. Margot's were brown."

"She had dimples around her mouth when she smiled," Micky observed.

"So did Jamie. I used to love it when he'd smile that teasing, half-laughing grin of his."

She handed several albums to Micky. "Let's take them into the kitchen."

Together they spread the albums on the table. "Here's one of Steve when he was only two."

A frowning baby in a wheelbarrow scowled up at her.

"He was miserable that day," Loretta remembered. She turned the page. "Here's one of Kent—and Jamie."

Excitement poured through Micky as she bent over it. Kent and Jamie stood facing the camera, smiling broadly. A hat was pulled low over Jamie's eyes, but she didn't miss his dimples lurking at the corners of his mouth. He was tall—like Jim—but not as broad.

"That was taken a few months before he left," Loretta explained. She glanced at the clock. "Goodness, it's seven-thirty already, and I told Louise I'd be there by eight. You can put the albums on my bed when you finish looking." She hurried away.

Micky turned the pages slowly: Steve dangling his first fish in the air; Kent's silhouette against the bank; Loretta stirring something over a camp stove; Margot dressed in a frilly, white dress.

Loretta popped back into the kitchen. She picked up an old navy blue album from the bottom of the stack, explaining, "I almost forgot. This is one I never let out of my sight."

Micky stared after her, a faint question forming in her mind. Was there something in that old album that Loretta didn't want her to see? Didn't want her to find out about?

No, she was being silly, imagining things. The phone rang and Micky hurried to answer it.

It was Tam. She came straight to the point. "I'm sorry, Micky. I was only teasing when I said you were coming to church just so Joel would date you. I didn't mean it—not really."

"Then you shouldn't have said it," Micky said tartly.

"I know. It was mean of me—really. Can you forgive me?"

Micky took a deep breath. "Is that what Joel thinks, too?" she asked.

"Of course not. You know how boys are. Even if they thought it, they wouldn't say it!"

"Did you tell Joel what you said to me?"

"Look, Micky. It was my own silly idea. I—"

"Did you tell Joel what you thought?" Micky persisted.

"Well—not exactly. But he doesn't think you're like

that, Micky. Really, he doesn't. Does it matter so much?"

"Yes, it does. I wish you hadn't, Tam."

"Oh, come on. I'm not perfect. We're still friends, aren't we?"

"I suppose," Micky said ruefully. "But next Sunday you don't need to come for me. I have someone else to take me to church."

As she put the receiver down, Micky wondered who it might be.

13

Steve Catches a Poacher

*T*am's teasing remark didn't keep Joel away after all. Saturday afternoon Micky heard his voice at the front door asking for her.

She flew out of the kitchen. Joel stood on the porch, brushing his shoes against the mat in front of the door, a small, light blue backpack perched high on his shoulders.

"Hi," he greeted. "I've got some hamburger patties. Want to go make a fire and help grill them?"

Micky's face brightened. "I've never done that," she said uncertainly.

"I've got matches, some condiments, and styrofoam cups. Got any hot chocolate mix?"

"I'll see." She hurried back into the kitchen. "Loretta, do we have any hot chocolate that I could take for a picnic? That is, if you don't mind . . ."

In a few minutes she reappeared, her cheeks flushed with enthusiasm. "I've got the chocolate mix, salt and pepper, and some hamburger buns!"

"Great!" He slung his pack from his shoulder and added her contributions.

"Where are you going to picnic?" Loretta asked.

"I thought that little grill above the whale hole—where we swim."

"But not today . . ."

Joel glanced through the window at the sunshine tracing leaf patterns on the lawn. "The sun's warm," he said, "but you're right, the water's too cold. But come July . . ."

They set out along the service road behind the hatchery. Micky took a deep breath, delighting in the stream rushing over mossy rocks, glinting gold and green in the sunshine.

"Someday I'd like to hike far enough to discover the stream's source," she said.

Joel smiled. "Me too." He glanced at her curiously. "You seem different today, Micky. Happier."

Micky's chin jerked. "I—"

Joel stopped. "You can tell me. What is it?"

A flush rose high in Micky's cheeks. "I wanted to— but Tam . . ."

Joel wore a puzzled smile. "Okay. What's my ever-lovin' sister been up to this time?"

"N-Nothing, really," Micky stammered. She tried to change the subject. "Come on. I'm starved."

Joel reached out and held her arm. "It must be something good—or you wouldn't look so happy. Come on," he entreated, "tell me."

Micky lowered her eyes and started walking. "I asked Jesus into my life Monday night," she whispered.

She looked up, unprepared for the joy that leaped into Joel's eyes. His hand tightened on her arm. "And you wanted me to be the first to know!" he cried. "That's wonderful—wonderful!"

"I know. It's just that I thought people might say I'd done it just so you would date me."

"That's nonsense!" Joel sputtered. "Where did you get such an idea?"

"Tam said—"

"What?"

"Right after I met you she said she thought you liked me but that you wouldn't date me unless I became a Christian." She bit her lip. "She said something on the phone that made me think she thought that was the reason I was going to church."

Joel frowned. "Is it?"

"At first it was, just a little bit," Micky explained bravely. "But after I'd gone a few times, I wanted to keep going no matter what."

Joel looked thoughtful. "Tam said something to me, too. She started teasing me about lowering my standards by dating a girl who wasn't a Christian. Funny, I hadn't even thought of our hiking along the creek or going to the May Day festivities as dates."

He caught her hand and grinned broadly. "Well, how about it? Want to go on a date? A real one?"

Micky stopped dead in her tracks. "Do you mean it?"

"Yes, I do."

Micky looked at him. There was a serious intent in his green eyes. This was no joke.

"I'd like to take you somewhere special," he continued, "partly to celebrate your new life, and partly because you're a very special girl."

A smile lit his entire face. He caught his lower lip between his teeth. "If you could choose a place to go, Micky, where would it be?"

Micky clasped her hands in front of her. "I'd like to dress up special and go to dinner—on the River Queen. Except—" she hesitated. "I guess that's sort of expensive."

Joel shook his head. "Doesn't matter. In a few days

I'll be helping roof the house Dad's working on. Besides, he already told me he'd finance a school's-out splurge." He spread his arms wide. "Fringe benefit, you understand. Let's plan it for Tuesday evening. I'll pick you up about five—"

"I'll ask Kent and Loretta."

"And so will I!" They laughed together as they headed up the hill. On one side of them the creek flashed and leaped; on the other, vine maple, ferns, and moss hung over their heads, transforming the high bank into a forest wonderland.

The road meandered farther up the hill, leaving the stream behind. But Joel and Micky detoured into a sun-drenched, grassy meadow, complete with a small grill. Joel slung his backpack beside it and joined Micky on the high bank overlooking the creek.

A narrow path veered down to the edge where a large rock jutted far out into the stream, forming a smooth, gray peninsula that reared upward into the air.

"Is that the whale?" Micky asked.

Joel nodded. "It's the only spot along here that's deep enough to swim in the summertime. It's fun to dive off the whale."

"This must be the place where the Middletons lost their daughter," she observed, noting the water swirling around the whale's head. "It looks safe enough. Maybe she misjudged and dived too wide—hit the shallows. I understand she was a strong swimmer."

A slight frown clouded Joel's eyes. "I'd almost forgotten." He looked at her. "Did you ever get an answer from the letters you sent to Spring Valley?"

"Yes. Paul Larson wrote. He said he'd lost contact with Jamie but was forwarding my letter to Jamie's last address. Later I wrote Jamie another letter telling him about my beginning a new life in Christ." She picked up a fallen stick and absently began pulling at the tiny fringes of dead moss.

"Something else happened, too, Joel. Peter Rabbit—I mean Jim—" She twisted a fragment of dead bark from her stick and tossed it into the stream. "He said something that made me think. . . . Could he be the Middletons' missing son, Jamie?"

"Jamie? That's impossible, Micky," Joel protested. "How could he be, so close-by and all, and Kent and Loretta not know it?"

"I saw Jamie's pictures in their photo albums," she insisted. "Jim could be him. Nine years have passed— he could be taller, heavier, and his beard would make him look a lot different." She giggled. "I'd like to see him without it—see if he has dimples at the corners of his mouth."

"But surely if the Middletons came face-to-face with him they'd know him."

"Probably. But yesterday Loretta was looking out the window when Jim walked by the road. She wanted to know who it was, and I explained it was my friend Jim from the hatchery. Then she sighed and said, 'Isn't it awful to have neighbors so close and not even know them?' "

Joel looked at her curiously. "What was it Jim said that made you think—"

"He was remembering—from his childhood. But of course, I could be mistaken." She shrugged. "Where do we get the water for the hot chocolate?"

Joel unzipped his pack and pulled out a water jug. A battered coffeepot followed.

Micky busied herself with the hamburger patties, seasoning them for the grill. Then she opened the mustard jar: "We forgot spoons, Joel!"

"We can use my knife."

"Or little sticks."

They scrambled through the underbrush in search of fallen branches for kindling. They returned, their arms full of deadwood.

Kneeling on one knee, Joel touched a lighted match to the dry fir needles. The flame caught, burning brightly.

"I could eat that hamburger raw," Joel admitted. The patties sizzled on the open grill while the buns toasted a light golden brown; steam rose from the coffeepot.

They sat with their backs braced against the smooth shoulder of a rock and ate their juicy burgers, relishing their own little world of warm sunshine, green grass, and the laughing creek.

When the sun withdrew from their sheltered nook, they stuffed the picnic remains into the pack and doused the fire. Reluctant to have their day end, they walked back slowly.

Instead of turning toward the pink house, they crossed the bridge below the hatchery and followed the stream downward.

Joel pushed a sagging branch aside. He nodded at the place where the young deer had been wedged beneath the water. "Remember Morning?"

Micky smiled. *Morning, the spirit of the creek—her tiny carving, the totem pole, Jamie . . .*

The sun was gone; the forest shadows beckoned no longer. But still Joel and Micky lingered, wandering farther and farther downstream. Joel stopped suddenly, his finger on his lips.

Micky peered around his broad shoulders; Steve

was crouched behind a log, staring intently at something just beyond their gaze.

Joel moved forward cautiously, and Micky followed. A twig snapped beneath her foot. Steve's head jerked, turning toward them.

Micky became really curious as she noticed a camera clutched tightly in his hand. She opened her mouth to ask him about it, then stifled it as he shook his head and made a wild pointing gesture downstream.

Two men on the bank below him were cutting open the bellies of two fish. Even in the dusk Micky saw the blood on their hands, the rosy eggs tumbling into their bucket.

Steve gestured to Joel and Micky to turn back. His mouth soundlessly articulated, "Call the po-lice."

Joel grabbed her hand. They bent low, slinking furtively beneath the bushes. When they were out of sight, they broke into a run.

"Telephone—" Joel gasped. "Your house—"

They headed for it, legs flying, hair blowing. Micky burst through the door and grabbed the phone. But there was no dial tone. Her finger pushed the button down—once, twice—no buzz, nothing. "It's dead!" she cried.

Joel grabbed the receiver from her ear. "You're right! Let's call from the hatchery—"

"No! Jim's house is closer."

They rushed out the door, down the road, across the grass, and onto Jim's porch. But there was no answer to Joel's frantic knocking. Micky pushed past him and shoved open the door. A telephone sat on a small desk. Micky picked up the receiver and handed it to Joel.

He dialed rapidly as Micky gasped for breath. Her

fingers nervously pushed back her hair, then toyed with the paperweight beside the phone.

"Police? We've got a poaching problem on Eagle Creek. Right below the hatchery."

Joel replaced the receiver and turned to her. "They'll have a car here in a few minutes. I'm going to the bridge to meet them."

He touched her shoulder gently. "You stay here. Explain to Jim." Then he was gone.

Micky turned the paperweight in her hands. It was a miniature totem pole. She was struck with awe as she touched the graceful deer, the trout, the soaring eagle.

She lifted her head. There was a comfortable-looking couch against one wall, covered with a colorful Indian blanket. A majestic painting of a bird darting beneath a waterfall hung over it, and green drapes were tied back to let in the outdoors. . . .

The back door opened and closed softly. She heard the sound of footsteps. Quickly, Micky replaced the totem pole on the pile of mail, but not before she saw her letter—addressed to Jamie.

She whirled around. Jim stood looking at her solemnly.

14

The Prodigal Son

Jim and a wildly excited Micky joined Steve, Joel, and the officer at the patrol car parked on the bridge. Steve's blue eyes sparkled. He flashed Micky a wide grin.

A strong satisfaction tingled deep inside her. *Catching those poachers will be good for Steve,* she thought. For the moment, she forgot the awful feeling when Jim had come in and found her staring at the papers on his desk. He still smiled, but a veil had come over his eyes. He looked different.

"This is my sister, Micky," Steve was saying. "And Jim, from the hatchery."

"Glad to meet you." The officer laid the completed papers inside the open car. "Your brother was the instigator of a fine bit of action," he told Micky. "He not only had this young man call us quickly, he also recorded the evidence with his pocket camera."

Joel grasped Steve's shoulder proudly. "No panic—just quick thinking. He did a great job."

"It was done in such a systematic fashion that it surprised me," the officer agreed. He slid behind the wheel, closing the door behind him. "Thanks to all of you!" he called.

The car was scarcely out of sight when Steve tossed

his camera wildly into the air. "Yippee!" he yelled. "Yippee!" He caught it and ran toward home.

Jim turned to Micky. "Proud of your brother?" he asked.

Hope flared within her. Had her intrusion been forgiven? She nodded. *And I'm proud of you, too,* she wanted to cry. *You came back, when you could have stayed away—forever.*

Instead she held out her hand. "I'm sorry about busting into your house like we did. But we needed to call—"

Jim smiled. His expression reminded Micky of a person caught between the present and a memory. He took Micky's hand. "It's all right," he said. But his eyes, which had once reminded Micky of deep wells of understanding, were still veiled.

Micky felt her eyes burn. "Good-night," she whispered.

Joel and Micky watched him walk away across the hatchery grounds.

"A man with a past," she murmured. "I wonder . . ."

Joel caught her hand. "Let's go to your house. I want to be in on the excitement when Steve tells Kent and Loretta about catching the poachers."

They hurried home. Loretta had apparently just returned, and she was listening intently as Steve regaled her with his tale.

"Why, Steve!" she marveled over and over.

"You should have seen their faces when I handed the cop the film from my camera," he boasted. "He said—"

"He was very outspoken in his praise of Steve," Joel interrupted. "He said he couldn't believe that one young boy could organize such an orderly plan of action."

Loretta shone, her excitement and pride equaling Steve's. "I can hardly wait to tell Kent," she whispered to Micky.

Goose bumps rose on Micky's arms. "Me either," she whispered, giving Loretta a hug.

"I wonder what's wrong with your telephone?" Joel wondered aloud.

The boys examined it. "The plug's pulled from the jack!" Joel exclaimed sheepishly. He looked at Micky, and they burst out laughing.

After a while, Joel left, but Loretta and Micky waited excitedly to share with Kent their pride in Steve's accomplishment.

Loretta popped a huge bowl of popcorn, and the three munched and talked until they heard a car roar down the hill.

Kent looked at them curiously as he came through the door. "What's up?" he asked.

"Steve has something to tell you, Kent," Loretta said. "He's had quite a day!"

When the details of the story were out, Kent, for once, seemed to be speechless. "Why, son," he kept repeating. "Why, son . . ."

Micky slipped out. Steve needed to be alone with his parents for a while. And she needed to be alone, too.

The flashing creek, the sizzling burgers, the sunshine warm on the boulder flashed like a kaleidoscope through her thoughts. With them came Joel's voice. "How about it? Will you date me?" Then, "Where to?" *The River Queen* . . .

Then another memory of the day came, tinged with confusion. Jim standing in the doorway of his house.

He'd only spoken two words, "Well, Micky?"

Shame had enveloped her, shame to be caught standing there looking at his mail. A flush had risen to her cheeks as she'd tried to explain . . . about the poachers, Steve, Joel, the telephone . . .

Quickly, Micky readied herself for bed. It wasn't until she was snuggled beneath her Indian blanket that she remembered her words to Tam:

"Don't bother to pick me up Sunday. I already have a ride."

Micky pushed the blanket back. Should she call Joel? She hesitated, stubborn pride restraining her.

Jim—would he take her? She knew she needed to talk to him, to break down the wall that had risen between them this afternoon.

She tossed on her robe and hurried down the stairs. The living room was dark. She turned on the lights and picked up the telephone, a prayer rising from her heart. *Lord, help me.*

"Jim?"

"Yes, Micky. What is it?"

But the words wouldn't come. She swallowed hard. "Could you—do something for me? Like take me to church in the morning?"

There was a long silence. Then a sigh. "Well, I'm not much of a church-going man, Micky. But for you . . ."

There was another long pause. Micky felt her heart thudding against her ribs.

"For you, Micky, I will. What time do we leave?"

Micky went back upstairs but not to sleep. After a while she opened her Bible to her favorite verses and began to read:

"As they were walking along the road, a man said

to him, 'I will follow you wherever you go.' Jesus replied, 'Foxes have holes and birds of the air have nests, but the Son of Man has no place to lay his head.' He said to another man, 'Follow me.' "

Micky smiled. "Yes, Jesus," she whispered, "I'll follow you anywhere. . . ."

That night Micky dreamed of a single mountain, still and white, stretching toward the sky. A single trail wound around and around it, and that was all there was to the dream.

She wakened with thoughts of single things. A bright red strawberry, a drop of water, a solitary leaf, a lonely eagle rising into the sky. One God, one Savior, the Mighty One.

She opened her eyes. The darkness had fled while she slept, and now the room was flooded with light. She watched a shaft of sunlight creep into the open closet door, slide down the sleeve of her white blouse, highlight her purple dress.

She got up and began pushing the hangers apart. She chose her soft pink-flowered dress and slid into it, feeling a tiny bit like a part of the morning. She held her hands out wide and whirled in a circle, wondering if Jim would be brave enough to come to the door for her.

She ran downstairs and into the kitchen—put bread into the toaster, raisin bran in her bowl. She poured milk on the cereal and sat down.

The doorbell rang while she was still eating. She shoved the bowl into the sink, grabbed her sweater, and opened the door.

Jim stood there, dressed uncharacteristically in a navy blue suit and matching tie. His dark hair was in place, his beard neatly trimmed.

Micky gasped. "I've never seen you . . . dressed up before, Jim. . . ."

Jim managed a smile. His nose twitched nervously. "Well, I don't have much occasion . . ." he said finally.

Micky quickly recovered her poise. *I hope I didn't frighten Peter Rabbit away when I burst uninvited into his home,* she thought. "You do look nice, Jim," she said, deliberately choosing to sidestep the awkwardness between them. "Has Mary ever seen you dressed up like that?"

Jim looked startled. "Who told you about Mary?"

"Steve. He told me you had a girlfriend. Is that right, Jim?"

Jim didn't answer. He strode on ahead and quietly opened the car door for her.

Micky tried to cover her distress with a constant patter of conversation. Jim didn't seem to be listening. At last she stopped trying and just looked at the scenery.

Once she stole a look at Jim's face. *He looks uncomfortable,* she thought. *Maybe I shouldn't have asked him to take me.*

At the church, a little old lady in a powder blue dress hurried up to them. "Why, Micky," she exclaimed, "you've brought your brother!"

Confusion clouded Micky's thoughts. She glanced at Jim. A strange look came over his face like a curtain. *He's thinking of Margot,* Micky thought.

"No," she said to the woman, smiling up at Jim. "But I wish he were."

Mr. Hoffman came over to them then, and Micky introduced the two men. Soon Mr. Hoffman was guiding Jim to the young adults class.

In Micky's classroom, Joel slid into a chair next to hers.

"How did you get here?" he asked.

"Jim brought me," she whispered.

A scowl wrinkled Joel's forehead.

"Aren't you glad?" she faltered.

Joel raised his eyebrows, silencing her questioning. Across the room, Tam smiled at her. It was an uncertain smile tinged with regret. Micky felt her pain. *I need to forgive her.*

It was hard to concentrate on Mr. Hoffman's words that morning. Micky's thoughts kept racing to the young adult class. Would they intimidate the shy Peter Rabbit with their eagerness and knowledge? Would Jim want to come again?

Micky slipped out of the classroom as soon as Mr. Hoffman dismissed them. She hurried to the foyer. Jim stood by a table, obviously looking for her.

She smiled and went over to him. "Shall we go inside?"

They found a place in the back pew, close by the door. Micky felt a pang of regret as she watched her own classmates squeeze together into a pew near the front. Joel was sitting close to an auburn-haired girl named Julie.

The music began. Micky began to sing, carefully concentrating on the words the way Mr. Hoffman had suggested they do. Her spirit lifted. She was singing to her Lord! She was His child!

The Scripture passage that morning was from the book of Luke. Micky caught her breath as the sweetness of the story of the lost son wrapped itself around her. She knew what it was to be lost and alone.

She glanced at Jim out of the corner of her eye. He seemed to listen intently, his eyes glued to Pastor Briggs.

" 'And he arose, and came to his father. But when he was yet a great way off, his father saw him, and had compassion, and ran, and fell on his neck, and kissed him.' "

Pastor Briggs laid his Bible on the pulpit and leaned forward. "I wonder if any of us can really comprehend the emotions that were going through that young man's heart, or those that the father felt on that day.

"This is the story Jesus told to illustrate to the tax collectors and sinners how much they were loved by God. The son was far from home. His friends were gone, he had nothing left that he could call his own. Yet his father loved him! He was watching, waiting, longing for him to come home. And when he did, he ran to meet him and hugged him and kissed him.

"It was a love big enough to forgive—big enough to risk everything for someone else."

Micky looked up at Jim's face. She was sure she saw tears in his eyes. She reached over and timidly touched his hand. He squeezed hers, then released it. "I have to go, Micky," he whispered. "I'm sorry . . ."

And he was gone. Micky felt tears form in her own eyes. *Oh, Jamie, come home, come home.*

For a moment she covered her face with her hands. "What is God saying to you right now?" Pastor Briggs asked. "That there's someone you need to forgive? Someone in your past that you're holding apart from, maybe even waiting for them to take the first step?"

Micky heard no more. *Tam!* her heart cried. Then, *Mother—Mother.*

15

I'm Michelle Ann Strand

*T*ears blurred Micky's eyes. The faces in the church foyer were blurred in a haze of colors.

Tam's long arms wrapped around Micky. "I'm sorry," she whispered, "me and my big mouth . . ."

Micky blinked hard. "I'm sorry too. After you called I didn't want to forgive you."

Tam leaned close. "Joel told me. We're sisters in Christ now."

"Sisters!" Micky's eyes widened. She looked at the people milling around her, heard their eager greetings, their laughter. "This is my new family!" she whispered.

Tam laughed with obvious delight. Joel joined them, taking Tam's arm. "Where is Jim?" he asked Micky.

"I don't know. I think the sermon got to him." She smiled weakly. "I know it got to me."

"Need a ride home?"

Micky swallowed hard. "Please."

After they let Tam out at a friend's house, Micky explained her reaction to the story of the Prodigal Son.

"For me it had to do with forgiveness," Micky said. "Ever since my mother left me I've been tangled up inside. First I'd hate her. Then I'd love her. Then I'd start over again—hating, loving, feeling bitter, resentful."

"And now?" Joel prodded.

Micky turned her dark eyes toward him. "Now, more than anything else, I want to forgive her," Micky said in a low voice. "And I think—I think it's something I have to do now."

She clasped her hands tightly in front of her. "I think I have to accept her as she is—with all her faults and weaknesses," her voice broke, "just like Jesus accepted me."

She turned to face him. "When I saw her at the hospital, I hated her for what she did—for leaving me, for running around, never satisfied.

"But even more, she frightened me. Would I grow up to be like her? Afraid to face responsibility? Always running from difficulties? from pain?"

Joel turned off onto a side road. Eagle Fern Park closed in around them; great firs and lofty maples rose on each side like a cathedral.

They got out of the car and walked over to a picnic table. They sat down with their backs braced against the table and looked at each other.

"Choosing to forgive your mother is a step in the right direction, Micky. But it's not humanly possible."

"I know. It's something I have to let Jesus do through me, isn't it?"

Joel nodded. "And since the Holy Spirit brought it to your attention, He'll give you the strength." He gently touched her hand.

"What I'm afraid of is that I won't say it right, Joel. Or that right in the middle, hate will overcome, and I'll make everything worse."

Joel sighed deeply. He looked up at the green canopy of leaves rustling over their heads. Micky had the feeling he was praying.

A chipmunk, growing suddenly bold, darted onto the edge of the table. Joel lowered his gaze, and the visitor with the bright, inquisitive eyes and the question mark tail dashed beneath the table.

Micky smiled. "Isn't he cute?"

Joel smiled. "Would it help if I went with you?" he asked. "I'd pray every minute, squeeze your hand if you even started to say something unkind."

Micky caught her breath, biting her lower lip. "Would you really?"

"Yes, I would. I'd consider it a privilege."

"Then," Micky said thoughtfully, "I think I'd like that."

She jumped up. The chipmunk scurried out from under the table and flashed up the fir, his tail arched, his angry chatter echoing through the park.

They laughed. "Funny little thing," Micky said. "I wish I had something to give him."

"We can come back another time. Maybe for a picnic." Joel caught her hand. "When should we see your mother?"

"I'm not sure. I'll have to call Mrs. Morton, find out where Mother is now."

———

But getting her mother's address wasn't as easy as Micky thought it would be.

"I'm sorry, Micky," the caseworker told her. "I don't have it. You could call the hospital. Maybe they'd give it to you."

But they wouldn't. "I'm sorry, but we don't give out that kind of information over the telephone. If you'd like to come in and talk to the supervisor . . ."

Micky put the receiver down, then called Joel.

"There's just one thing to do, Micky," he said. "We'll go to the hospital—together."

It was hard for Micky to enter the busy reception room, harder still to be ushered into a tiny room and told to wait. Through the open door, the loudspeaker crackled, "Dr. Molaski, Dr. Molaski, please." Micky clutched Joel's hand, a metallic taste rising in her throat.

A smiling woman in a black skirt and deep purple blouse hurried into the room. "I'm Mrs. McAllister, administrative assistant. May I help you?"

Micky licked her lips. "It's about a patient who was here a month ago: Joanne Cochran. I'd like her address."

"Just a moment." Mrs. McAllister left the room and came back carrying a folder. She leafed through it, her long, slim hands efficient. When she looked up, her quick glance was impersonal. "I'm sorry. She left specific instructions not to give her address to anyone."

Micky suddenly sat forward, squaring her shoulders. "But I'm not just anyone," she said. "I'm her daughter, Michelle Ann Strand. I have every right to know where she is."

The woman raised an eyebrow. She looked at Micky intently, then turned toward the door. "Another minute, please . . ."

Joel put his arm around Micky's shoulder. "Good for you, Micky," he whispered. His arm tightened. "Michelle Ann Strand." The way he rolled it on his tongue made it sound beautiful.

Tears stung Micky's eyes and she blinked. She opened her purse and took out a tissue.

Mrs. McAllister came back with a piece of paper. She handed it to Micky. "Your mother was discharged to this address ten days ago. Good luck."

Micky thanked her, and she and Joel hurried to the car. "Do you think we can find it?" Micky asked uncertainly. "It's on Northeast Hoyt Street."

Joel was unconcerned. "We've got all afternoon."

It almost took them that long to find it. They discovered dead-end streets; one-ways, going the wrong way; detours for street repairs; not to mention misread signs and wrong turns.

At last, a shabby gray house on a busy corner revealed the number the woman had given them. They parked on the street and ascended a narrow flight of steps along the outside of the house.

"This can't be it, can it?" Micky muttered, observing the sagging rail, the dingy curtains covering the windows. The hard ache in her throat was back, worse than before. "Oh, Joel. What an awful place to come when you're sick—and down."

Joel knocked, but there was no answer. A vast emptiness seemed to envelop them. He knocked again, with no response.

Micky sat down on the steps. She looked up at Joel. "I could write her a letter and leave it here!"

Joel nodded and ran to the car for a pad of paper. He pressed it into her hands with a stub of a pencil.

Micky's fingers were cold and she didn't know what to write. "I don't know what to say!"

Joel joined her on the steps, his long legs stretching beyond hers. "Just follow your heart, Micky. Follow your heart."

But the words wouldn't come. Desperately, Micky chewed on the end of the pencil. Joel patted her shoulder and stood up. "I'll be back in a little while."

Micky watched the car move away—noted Joel's encouraging smile, his quick wave. Then he was gone.

The rush of tears she'd been fighting for so long broke loose. Sitting alone on the gray, battered steps, Micky wept—for her mother and her father, for all the happiness they might have had, for the years that were lost.

When she'd regained her composure, she began to write:

Dear Mother,

I love you and want to say I'm sorry—for blaming you, for hating you.

The reason I can say it now is because I have a new life. It's because of a person—the Lord Jesus Christ.

I wanted to see you again. Maybe another time.

Your daughter,
Micky

She pushed it under the door and ran down the steps. Joel had pulled his car up to the curb, and she hopped inside.

"We're going to picnic at the park with our chipmunk and—Colonel Sanders."

The smell of the fried chicken made Micky's mouth water. She smiled. "Let's go," she agreed. "I'm hungry."

———

That night Micky dreamed she was in a canyon, surrounded by high, reddish bluffs. Peter Rabbit walked toward her. "So you are Michelle Ann Strand," he said, "Michelle Ann Strand."

His voice echoed off the canyon walls, "Michelle Ann Strand." "Michelle Ann Strand . . ."

Micky wakened suddenly, the walls reverberating

with her name. Fear encompassed her. It took her a moment to realize it was only a part of a dream.

She turned on the light. The walls were the familiar, comforting knotty pine, not high, impregnable red rock.

I must talk to Jim, she thought, *tell him about my note to Mother.*

Her eyes wandered to the queen's bouquet she'd hung above her mirror. The flowers were dried now, the white eyelets of the baby's breath still lovely.

"Michelle Ann Strand," she whispered, "Joel said it was a beautiful name."

As soon as the family had left next morning, Micky hurried to the hatchery. It took her a while to find Jim. He was beyond the bridge, on his knees, repairing a broken water main. He looked up.

"About yesterday, Jim—"

Jim put the pipe down and reached into his back pocket, pulling out a rag. He wiped his hands, then stood.

"I shouldn't have left you at the church the way I did, Micky. It wasn't very kind, that's for sure. But I figured your boyfriend would give you a ride home."

A blush rose to Micky's cheeks. Jim already considered Joel her boyfriend. "I'm not blaming you, Jim. I only wanted you to know that I understand."

Haltingly, stumbling over her words, Micky told him about her own reaction to the story of the Prodigal Son. She told him of her subsequent search for her mother that resulted in finding an empty apartment in a run-down neighborhood.

"It would have meant a lot if I could have seen her, Jim, asked her face-to-face to forgive me, but I couldn't. I did leave her a note, though."

Jim was quiet for a long moment, shifting the wrench from hand to hand. "But, Micky," he said at last, "you went and asked for forgiveness. You tried to make things right." He laid the wrench beside the pipe, then slowly straightened. "Do you think that if you go away from your home, your family, the place you spent your childhood, even if you come back, do you ever really find it again?"

Micky thought about it. "I think in some ways you'll be hunting for it all your life," she said. "But if you find God—"

Jim reached out a grimy hand and patted her shoulder. "You're a good girl, Micky. And I—I'm still nothing but a wimp." He shook his head. "I don't have any courage—no courage at all. And I'm afraid to trust God with my past."

With that, he simply turned and walked away. Micky stared after him, then went back to the house.

After her morning chores were finished, she picked up her Bible and went outside to the hammock beneath the birch trees. This morning the trees were whispering, dipping, and swirling. *Like ballerinas,* Micky thought, *with the masculine dark firs towering protectively over them.*

Micky lay back in the hammock. The sun spangling through the leaves reminded her of the sequins that danced on the creek, shooting out miniature rainbows.

She opened her Bible and began to read the stories of the lost coin, the lost sheep, and the lost son.

Her thoughts began to scatter, like water spray against the rocks. She jumped suddenly—something of heavy glass seemed to fall and burst into a thousand pieces.

"I didn't mean to wake you," Loretta was saying.

Micky sat up. "You didn't. I guess I was dozing a little. I heard a pitcher or something breaking."

She rubbed her eyes, then looked up at Loretta; her face was white, her mouth moving to speak, but no words came out. Micky leaped to her feet.

"Loretta!" she cried, "what is it?"

Loretta sank into a lawn chair and Micky dropped to her side.

"I got a telephone call at work. It was about your mother . . ."

An icy coldness swept over Micky and her face drained of color.

"She's dead, isn't she."

Loretta nodded, tears filling her eyes, then trailing down her cheeks.

Micky's eyes burned but there were no tears.

"I'm so sorry, Micky," Loretta whispered.

"Sorry? Why are you sorry? She was my mother. . . ." Micky hated the sound of her own voice, so unfeeling, so mechanical. "How could God let it happen?" she said woodenly. "Just when I was ready to love her—to care about her . . ." She jumped to her feet.

"Micky, wait! I need to tell you the rest . . ."

But Micky was already running—away—toward the beckoning tall firs and the solitude they offered.

16

Younger Sister

*T*he hazel brush slapped Micky's arms. Overhanging blackberry vines clawed at her hair, twisted at her ankles.

Deeper and deeper into the heart of the woods she ran. The burning pain in her spirit turned into a searing pain in her lungs, her breath coming in ragged gasps.

She caught her foot in a vine maple crawling along the forest floor and went sprawling. Rather than try to get up, Micky buried her face in the pungent green moss, her hands knotting into fists. She pounded the soft, yielding blanket beneath her. "Oh, God!" she cried. In her despair she thought of the tender moss being crushed, pummeled, and beaten just like she was. "Oh, God!"

She rolled onto her back and looked up. The sunshine turned the upper tree trunks into shades of gray, from light to dark, accentuating the tiny moss clusters.

"God," she whispered, "couldn't you have just let me say I was sorry to her?"

Bitterness held back the tide of tears. "You're mean—poison mean, just like Jamie said you were. Did you really have to take her now—just like that?"

There was a flash of blue high in the branches. Micky closed her eyes. A bird trilled, a chipmunk scolded, a crow cawed in the distance, softening its harsh tones.

Slowly she became aware of a soft rustling around her. The vine maple leaves trembled in a stray breeze.

"Trust Me," they seemed to whisper. "Just trust Me."

Nearby alders took up the refrain. "Trust Me . . . trust Me . . ."

Then a new song, "I love you. I love you. I love you."

The pain dammed up inside Micky's heart was suddenly released. "Oh, God," she cried through burning tears, "I love you. I trust you. Forgive me."

It was several hours before Loretta, weary, scratched, and dirty, found Micky. Her head pillowed on the moss, she was sound asleep, tear marks still on her cheeks.

Loretta sank down beside her. She smoothed back her tangled hair and wiped the dusty tears from her face. "My little girl," she whispered. "My very own little girl."

Micky stirred and opened her eyes. For a moment her dark eyes were peaceful. Then memory returned. "Oh, Loretta—"

Loretta wrapped her arms around her, gently drawing her close. Micky snuggled her face into her lap. The bushes resumed their gentle whisperings of trust— love—trust. A woodpecker flew onto a maple limb and observed the pair curiously.

"There's something I need to tell you, Micky," Loretta finally said. "Your mother—" She paused, her voice quavering with tension. "Your mother—was my sister."

Bewilderment and disbelief showed on Micky's

face. "What? I don't understand."

Loretta's lips trembled. "It isn't easy to explain, Micky . . ."

Micky sat up and rested her head on Loretta's shoulder. "I want to hear about it."

Loretta took a deep, wavering breath and began. "It's a long story. But you need to know . . .

"There were just the two of us—Joanne and I. She was the older—eager for life, happy, alive. I was the quiet one, the ordinary one who always craved attention.

"I loved your mother, but it was hard—especially when she always seemed to get just what she wanted and then, just as easily, she'd throw it away.

"She was that way with men, too. She was attractive, and they liked her. But as soon as she had their devotion, she'd cast them aside. And I couldn't even get a man to look at me."

"But—you and Kent . . ." Micky protested.

A dark shadow crossed Loretta's face. "This was before Kent, Micky.

"To make a long story short—we drew apart, your mother and I. I hated it when I heard she'd left you— to think she could take motherhood so lightly. It seemed so unfair! And I always seemed to be in her shadow— waiting for life—for love."

Micky suddenly sat up straight. "You knew who I was, then!" she cried.

"No, Micky. I didn't know—not at first."

"But why didn't you tell me, when you did know!"

"I didn't even tell Mrs. Morton, Micky! I was afraid being Joanne's sister, with her reputation, would jeopardize my being considered for your foster parent. And I wasn't taking any chances on losing you."

"But why didn't you take me right away—when Daddy couldn't, before I became a ward of the court?" Memories of the many foster homes flashed before Micky's eyes: the endless round of new faces, new siblings, new bedrooms, new schools—the voices: *Micky, you can't do that—we don't allow that. Micky! Micky! Why are you always running away?*

"I lost track of you when Joanne left your father," Loretta broke in to Micky's thoughts. "I didn't know you didn't have a home. Not until I saw you with Mrs. Morton. No one ever told me!"

Micky nodded. "They looked for my mother, too, and they couldn't find her. They told me that once." She looked up at the alder trees glinting gold in the slanting rays of sunshine. "Does Kent know I'm your niece?"

"No. I never told him."

Loretta grew quiet, seeming not to want to talk any longer. Micky noticed her fingers tightly clasped into fists, the dark circles beneath her eyes. Loretta had lost a sister. Maybe not a dearly loved one, but a sister just the same.

Compassion stirred in Micky. She knew the hurt of painful love twisted with regret.

She touched Loretta's clenched hand. "I'm so sorry, Loretta. To lose someone you loved—even long ago—someone you grew up with . . ."

Tears misted Loretta's eyes. "Not as long ago as you think, my darling. I went back to the hospital alone, after I took you. I have you to thank for giving Joanne and I those last weeks together."

She unclenched her fists and touched Micky's cheek. "We got to know each other better—to understand. I even talked to her about you. She hung on to every word . . ."

A tide of bitterness rose up in Micky again. "Then how could you have let her be discharged to that awful apartment?" she whispered.

"I had to," Loretta murmured. "I had no choice . . ." She got up and held out her hand. "Come on, Micky, let's go home."

Home! It was a sweet sound to Micky's ears. She held out her hand and allowed Loretta to pull her to her feet.

"Loretta!" Micky cried, the realization dawning on her. "You're my aunt! My real Aunt Loretta! And Kent's my uncle—and Steve—"

Loretta squeezed her hand. It was her only answer.

———

That night when the house was quiet, Micky thought about all that had happened in the past twenty-four hours. Yes, her Lord had allowed her mother to be taken from her, but He'd given her an aunt to love her, a lovely home by a magical stream that whispered and wooed, a warm church family—Joel, Tam, and—Jim, her own dear Peter Rabbit.

Micky sat upright in bed. "Jamie," she whispered. "Jim. He's Loretta's stepson. That means I have another cousin!"

She laughed out loud, hugging her knees with her arms. "My cousin—my friend . . ."

She jumped up and pulled out paper and pen from her desk drawer. The lamp burned late as Micky wrote down her thoughts—she would tell Jamie about the fact that her mother and his stepmother were sisters. She would tell him they were cousins. She'd ask him to come home—soon.

The day Joanne was buried was a golden day. The scent of flowers blew through the cemetery; the breeze wiped the cheeks of the mourners gathered beside the plain pine box.

The minister's words were few, his prayer simple. But Micky scarcely heard them. She stood beside her Aunt Loretta and thought how quickly the past dissolved into the future, and unfulfilled dreams were quietly laid aside.

Afterward, a woman in a soft lilac dress put her hand on Micky's arm. "You must be Michelle," she said softly.

Micky looked at the woman's round face filled with compassion and concern, the gentle, childlike blue eyes.

"How did you know my name?" Micky asked.

"Your mother told me about you. She was only in her apartment above me a few days before they took her to the nursing home. I found the note you left under the door. I thought it might be important, so I took it to the home. I read it to her that night—before she died."

The compassionate face crumpled, and a tear coursed down the woman's wrinkled face.

She looks like a faded rose, Micky thought. *She must have been beautiful when she was young.* She put her arm around the drooping shoulders.

"I'm so glad you gave her my note," she said earnestly. "More than anything I wanted her to know that I forgave her—that in spite of everything, I loved her."

The woman's lips trembled. "It meant a lot to her, I know. I'll never forget the way she clung to my hand

and thanked me over and over, but I never dreamed it would be her last night."

Neither did I, Micky thought.

As the woman walked away, Micky wandered across the grassy cemetery and read some of the markers. One without a name said simply: "God's lamb—the Lord took him." The stone next to it read: "Constance Harding—Christian, wife, mother."

Micky's eyes smarted. *It must be a mother and child.* A sudden movement just beyond the edge of the lot caught her attention. She stepped around a sweet-scented lilac bush.

A man strode away into the distance, his dark head held high. Micky caught her breath. Was it Jim? But it couldn't be. Wasn't he off tending fish tanks and water mains?

She opened her mouth to call him, but thought better of it. If he wanted to be near her in her grief, and remain unseen, that was his privilege. She wondered vaguely if he'd ever met his Aunt Joanne.

Micky reached for a lilac branch and breathed in the sweet perfume. It probably wasn't Peter Rabbit anyway.

17

The Whale

This morning I'm noticing how often Abraham stood before his Lord—praying, listening, Micky wrote. *I'm learning a little bit about that too—how to listen, how to pray.*

Micky stuck her pen behind her ear and smiled at the dancing cherry leaves all around her. Keeping a spiritual journal was becoming an important part of her life. It was something Mr. Hoffman, her Sunday school teacher, had suggested she do.

Sometimes she wrote down a special verse, sometimes an observation or a thought that seemed important. Micky liked the way it was helping to change her.

Like the cherry tree, she thought, fingering her notebook, *first there are the blossoms, then the ripening fruit, and now green leaves absorbing the sunshine, preparing for winter and another season . . .*

She turned to a new section entitled NATURE. She had copied the idea from the old scrapbook Jamie had left on the closet shelf. Stuffed with everything from animal track patterns to his own observations, it contained a wealth of information.

Already, Micky's own notebook was filling with magazine clippings, jottings from her daily woodland walks, pressed flowers and leaves. It was always close-by. Everyone in the family teased her about it, especially Kent.

"For a girl who hates school, you sure take the cake. Magazines, books, and that notebook." He'd gone off grumbling, but Micky knew he was pleased with her interest in reading, writing, and noticing the things of nature.

———

Joel was pleased too. Dinner on the *River Queen* had been a special occasion, a summer highlight. But it was rambling up and down the creek together, searching out crayfish, fingering beetles, bits of lichens, that had been the heart of summer.

July had come in with a bang. Micky'd seen the blazing fireworks display at Oaks Park on the Willamette River with Joel, Tam, and her boyfriend. It had gone out with a glorious lightning display ripping through the giant thunderclouds, and claps of thunder keeping her awake.

It was August now, with Queen Anne's lace decorating the roadside and white thistledown blowing high on the breeze. Soon school would begin. In spite of the fears that clouded her anticipation, Micky knew she wanted to go.

She took a deep breath, and thought about thick fall sweaters, school clubs and classrooms, football, biology. Her fingers itched to grasp a microscope, explore the parts of a flower, peer into a bit of pond water . . .

But sometimes she wondered: Would the trauma of a new school situation, new classmates, new teachers, be worth going through for the sake of the activities and classes?

Occasionally she thought of her mother, but not often. Only once had she been overwhelmed by her feelings. That was when she found, tucked inside the pages of Jamie's old scrapbook, a picture of her mother—young, happy, so very much alive.

Micky gathered her Bible and notebook and crawled to the window. Before climbing inside, she moved a leafy branch and looked down at the hatchery.

She knew something awful was bothering Jim. She missed their comfortable comradery, their long talks. A pang of realization shot through her: He'd been avoiding her.

She sensed it was more than his discovering her at his desk on the evening Steve had caught the poachers. Maybe he felt uncomfortable with the long letters she faithfully wrote him each week, the bits and pieces she shared about her new family.

Micky dropped the branch and climbed in the window. She grabbed her swimsuit, towel, and terry coverup. Passing the mirror, she was pleased with the look of her tanned legs and arms in contrast to her light blue shorts and T-shirt. Long, lazy hours on the whale rock and frequent dips in the stream were responsible. She dashed downstairs.

"Steve!" she called. "Let's go for a swim!"

The clock above the stove read 1:30. "He said he'd go down with me at one-thirty," she muttered.

She waited a half hour for him, busying herself with straightening the living room. Then she became restless and wondered if Steve could have gone on ahead. She picked up her swimming gear and headed up the road, past the hatchery, to the stream.

The August sun was hot on her shoulders. In spite of her irritation with Steve, she was enjoying the prospect of a good swim. Arriving at the rock, Steve was nowhere to be seen. The grassy meadow with the grill was empty, and the whale was bare.

Micky slipped into the leafy glade, which served as a dressing room, and changed into her navy and white suit and brief terry coverup. Draping her towel over her arm, she went down the narrow path, across the small rocks, and up the whale head.

She spread her towel on the flat top of the rock's head and lay down, the sun hot on her bare skin. She wished Steve would hurry up.

The water lapped around the rock, cool and inviting. Micky stood up, went to the lower edge, and ventured an exploring toe. Ahh! this was the life.

She cast off her terry wrap, lowered her foot, and began to wade into the deeper water. *I shouldn't swim alone,* she thought.

"Just once won't matter," she muttered. "Steve should be here any minute, anyway." Quietly, the stream drew her in. A warm breeze swirled the waters around her and urged her farther and farther from shore. As she went in deeper, the water was colder and felt good against her warm skin. Soon she was swimming, then floating on her back.

Then, without warning, a sharp pain clenched her stomach into a knot. She panicked. "Help! Help!" she cried. Desperately trying to keep her head above water, the pain, mingled with the current and her own fear, drew her down. Her lungs burned, and then everything was dark.

She was hardly aware of the strong arms pulling her to the surface. She gasped and choked and spit water. Then the rocky shore pressed into her side, and she felt someone cover her with her terry wrap and towel. She opened her eyes. The trees wavered, then stilled. Jim's face came into focus.

His finger touched her cheek. "Don't cry, Micky." But she rolled onto her stomach, pressed her face into her hands, and let the tears flow.

Jim lifted her into his arms. "I'm taking you home."

Micky didn't argue. She rested her head on his shoulder and trembled like a leaf. Her teeth chattered uncontrollably.

Jim hurried down the path, whispering soothing words to her. His steps were firm, his arms strong and caring. Micky knew Peter Rabbit was her friend again.

He hesitated at the gate. Loretta was running to open it, looking terrified. "Micky! Micky! What happened?"

Steve was right behind her. "Is she all right?"

Kent came around the corner of the house, dropped his shovel, and motioned Jim toward a reclining lawn chair. "Put her here, young man."

Gently, Jim laid Micky in the chair and spoke to her again. "It's all right, Micky, You're home now."

He turned to Kent. "I pulled her out of the whale hole up yonder. I think she's okay, though."

Loretta covered Micky with a blanket and went to get her something hot to drink.

Micky swallowed hard and looked at Kent and Jim. They just stood and stared at each other, neither one speaking. Did Kent know he was looking at his son?

She blinked hard. She didn't know if she saw tears in Kent's eyes or if it was the water in her own. She closed them for a moment, and when she opened them again, Kent and Jim were in a strong embrace.

Micky knew then that she would always remember

Kent's words: "My son, my son. You've come home. Thank God, you've come home."

She couldn't remember when she'd felt so happy.

And when Loretta came out of the house, she gasped and fell into Jim's arms, sobbing like a child.

Micky pulled Steve close, explaining, "It's Jamie, their lost son—your brother."

"But—" Steve shook his head. "How could it be?" he asked.

"I've known for some time," Micky admitted.

Steve scowled at her. "And you didn't tell me?"

"I didn't tell anyone."

"Wow! I can't believe it! And he saved your life, Micky," Steve told her.

"I know, Steve, I know. Peter Rabbit is my hero."

———

Later that evening, Kent, Loretta, Steve, and Micky gathered in the living room. Micky was the center of attention.

"So you knew all the time that Jim was Jamie!" Loretta marveled.

"Well, not all the time. But the totem pole reminded me of something Jim would like, and then I found the note."

"The totem pole?" Steve said, puzzled.

"What note?" Kent asked.

"I put it in the totem pole."

Loretta flew up the stairs and brought it down.

Micky carefully unscrewed the base while Kent and Steve looked on. She pulled the note out and laid it on the coffee table. "I found it in back of the bookshelves, wedged behind the baseboard. It said he went to Spring Valley, so I started writing there.

"But it wasn't until I saw the letter I'd written to Jamie on Jim's desk, the night Steve caught the poachers, that I knew for sure."

"He's grown that beard," Loretta mused, "and he's taller and broader now. It makes me feel bad that I didn't recognize him earlier."

"But you never saw him up close until today," Kent consoled. "If you had, you would have known him."

"I'm not so sure," Loretta said. "He's changed. He's a grown man now."

"And a hero!" Steve exclaimed. "To pull Micky out of the stream like that—"

"But he was afraid," Micky said softly. "He told me that." Everyone was quiet, hanging on her every word. "He's blamed himself and hated himself all these years because of his fear of the water and what happened to Margot."

Kent nodded. "He told me he froze when he saw you, Micky, going off alone to the swimming hole. Then he said, 'I had to follow her, to face my fears once and for all.' "

Kent put his arm around Micky. "If he hadn't, you wouldn't be here—" His voice broke.

Steve's fingers traced the design of the totem pole. "I'm proud of my brother," he said, "proud of his carvings, his work at the hatchery. But most of all, I'm proud that he looked his fear in the face. . . . Someday . . ."

Micky waited expectantly. But Steve said no more.

Everyone has some kind of fear to face up to, Micky thought. *Steve has his fear of heights, I'm afraid of being rejected at school . . .*

She looked at Steve. Already, since she'd been with the Middletons, he'd grown. His ankles stuck out awkwardly below his blue jeans. Now there was new purpose shining from his blue-gray eyes. Micky had a feeling Steve's someday would be soon.

———————

That night Micky lay in bed, too restless to sleep. The day's events whirled through her mind: the cold water sucking her beneath the surface, Jim pulling her out and carrying her home. . . . She never could have dreamed that Jim's reunion with his family would come about like it did.

Just before Jim left, he'd pulled her aside. "I'm going to call Mary," he whispered, "tell her I've come home."

"I'm glad," Micky had responded. "She needs to know what I've known all the time—that you have real courage."

There had been a knowing response in Jim's eyes. He left them all walking taller than ever, his head held high. Even now, Micky could see him in her mind's eye.

Her bedroom door opened softly, and Micky's heart leaped. "Who is it?"

"Micky," Loretta whispered, "are you awake?"

"Yes." Micky propped herself up on one elbow. "What is it?"

Loretta came close to the bed, and Micky reached for the light switch, but Loretta stopped her. "No," she said, "that won't be necessary.

"Micky, your mother asked me not to tell you something. But now—since Jamie's return, and your accident—I feel you have a right to know. That it would be important to you. I'm putting something here on your nightstand. After I leave, turn on your lamp. I think you'll understand."

Her fingertips touched Micky's cheeks. "We'll talk in the morning."

Then Loretta went out as softly as she'd come. Micky waited until she heard the door close at the bottom of the stairs. Her fingers groped for the light switch.

Loretta had left a family picture. Micky immediately recognized her mother and Kent. But the two children with them? She turned the picture over: Jamie—age 6, Margot—age 4.

Micky caught her breath as she bent over the portrait. Kent and her mother—both so happy, so young. Together.

18

Mother's Secret

*M*icky looked at the cedar encircled enclosure; the spreading limbs before her formed a triangular opening partially blocked with a low-growing vine maple. Inside, a soft indentation in the earth marked the outline of a large animal's body.

"Is this really a deer's bedding place?" Micky asked with awe.

Joel nodded. "Yes, that soft, hollowed-out spot. I call it 'Morning's nesting place.' "

Micky looked at him. "You think about her too?"

"Sure. I guess I'll always think of her when I see a young doe. Maybe that's why I thought it was so great to find this."

"Morning's place."

"Yeah, if it is Morning's!"

"I think it might be," Micky said wistfully.

"When I first found it early one morning, it was still warm. She must have just left." He held out his hand.

Micky took it in hers, and they started up the hill, then turned to look back. Micky could picture Morning's pixy face peering through the leaves, the flip of her white tail as she turned to run.

Farther along, the trees parted, and the two hiked

to the crest of a bluff. The hatchery, with its shimmering waterways, spread beneath them, soaking up the midday sun. The creek, slim and silver, rushed silently, muted by the distance.

All of a sudden, Micky understood why the stream was called Eagle Creek. Remote, wild—holding its admirers just a bit distant—yet wondrously beautiful and alive.

Micky's face was flushed and her dark hair clung to her temples with the moisture. She stepped back into the shade of a giant fir and sat, her legs stretching down the grassy slope.

She smiled up at Joel, pleased to have conquered the climb, but a little breathless, too. "What do you think?" she asked. "Nice picnic place, huh?"

Joel looked around the clearing. "Perfect." He walked over to a long, narrow boulder and sat down. "We could bring up a small grill with no problem." He bent down, examining the rock. "There's a little hollow that goes way under here. We could keep a coffeepot inside it."

"Wouldn't my totem pole look great up here on top? I can just imagine it sitting here—high above the creek."

"But the weather would ruin it," Joel warned.

"I know," Micky sighed. "It's only a dream. Actually, I'm going to keep it in my room always—to remember."

Joel slid off the rock and sat down beside Micky. They were silent for a moment. A quail drummed somewhere in the woods; a bird close-by gave a surprising little squawk; there was a faint humming buzz. The end of summer was evident all around them.

"I went swimming with Steve yesterday," Micky said.

"Oh, how was it?"

Micky leaned back into the warm sunshine. "It was special, Joel."

She sat up again, pulling her knees forward, wrapping her tanned arms around them. "As soon as he asked me to go with him, I knew he had something on his mind. But it wasn't until we got to the whale that he told me.

"He asked me to just be there while he dove off the whale—alone." Her dark eyes sought Joel's. "He's afraid of heights, you know . . .

"Anyway, he asked me to cover my eyes. So I did. Except I peeked! Joel, he stood on that rock—trembling. Then he dove in.

"There should have been a band playing, and cheers going up; it was such an accomplishment for him. But there was just me, and I wasn't supposed to be looking."

A proud glow filled her eyes. "He's different now, Joel. He looks his father in the eye and stands up straight."

"And Jim—Jamie," Joel added. "He's different, too, since he pulled you out of the water."

Micky nodded. She picked up a twig and began breaking it into little lengths, stacking them neatly. Joel began to lay them in the pattern of a little bonfire. He looked up.

"Micky, something's changed you, too. And I don't think it was just Jamie's coming home."

Micky nodded. "Loretta shared my mother's secret with me, that night after I almost drowned."

She took a deep breath. "She came into my room

and left a family portrait on my bed, for me to look at alone after she left the room. It was a picture of Kent, my mother, Jamie and Margot when they were small . . ."

"What!" Joel exclaimed.

"That's what I thought! The next morning Loretta told me the whole story. But first, you need to know that Loretta had already told me, after my mother died, that Joanne was her older sister!"

"Sisters! Then that makes you and Jamie cousins!"

"Wait—there's more. Years ago, before I was even thought of, my mother was married to Kent. Unwilling to handle her responsibilities of two small children, she took off. I guess Kent was a difficult husband, too—hard to please."

Micky shrugged. "Anyway, she left. Later there was a divorce, a lot of hurt and bitterness, and Kent was left alone with the two children. When Loretta offered to take them, Kent, not knowing how to care for them, was relieved. Loretta said she hated her sister for taking being a mother and a wife so lightly. She had everything Loretta had ever longed for and had merely tossed it aside.

"More and more Kent turned to Loretta, and she grew to love him deeply. When he asked her to marry him, she was more than ready to say yes."

"But why wouldn't your mother have wanted you to know all that?" Joel questioned. "It doesn't make sense."

"That's what I said to Loretta! But when Mother was in the hospital, she begged Loretta not to tell me, that she was ashamed of the way she'd left both her families and deeply regretted it."

"But she took your brothers!"

"That's what I thought. But she didn't keep them! Someday soon I'm going to talk to Mrs. Morton—see if I can find them. Mother confided in Loretta; she said the authorities wouldn't let her see them—because of the emotional scars she'd inflicted on them."

Micky's dark eyes filled with tears. "Joel, do you know how wonderful it is to have the Lord at a time like this? Someone you can count on, who'll never let you down?"

"Yes, but probably not in the same way you do. Micky, did Kent know about the natural relationship between you and Loretta?"

"No, not until Loretta told him—the same night she told me. Looking back, I can see that I probably reminded Kent of Margot—our eyes and smiles are somewhat alike—and that's what's frustrated him so. But Loretta kept it all to herself—until Jamie came home."

"Jamie! Micky, he's your half brother!"

Micky nodded. "That's why Loretta wanted me to hear the whole story. She felt I had a right to know my own brother.

"I feel the Lord has given me a very special gift. All my life I've wished for a big brother. And Jim, well—he's been that from the first, and I never even knew we were related. When I thought he was my cousin, I was delighted—and now to find he's even closer! It's one of those 'more than you even ask or think' surprises from the Lord."

"And to think, I was sort of jealous of him—" Joel admitted.

"You—jealous? Of Jim?"

Joel grinned. "Oh, just a little. Sometimes I wondered. You seemed so close."

"We were—we are." Micky stood and walked to the edge of the bluff.

Her world lay before her, cradled in a giant cup. She almost wished she could stay here, keep the challenges at a safe distance. But she couldn't. Jamie had faced his fears, saving her from the water he dreaded. Steve had conquered his fear of heights. Even Kent and Loretta were making peace with their past.

"Joel," she said, "I'm looking forward to going back to school. I know it'll be hard, my being behind a year and all. But I'm going to face it head on."

Joel stood behind her, his hands clasping her arms. "But Micky," he whispered, "you won't be alone. I'll be there too."

His hands tightened. Micky could feel his breath against her hair. "Micky, I'm looking forward to seeing you in the grandstands cheering me on during the football season."

He paused. "And one other thing, Michelle Ann Strand, will you be my girl?"

Micky took a deep breath, then turned to him. "Yes, Joel," she whispered, "I would be very happy and proud to be your girl friend."

If you enjoyed this book, look for these other young adult novels by Bethany House Publishers at your local bookstore:

New Girl in Town by Judy Baer
Book one in the exciting CEDAR RIVER DAYDREAMS series. Lexi Leighton discovers that making friends in her new home town is next to impossible—until she gets a date with the most sought-after guy in town. But will she have to compromise her ideals in order to keep him?

Too Many Secrets by Patricia H. Rushford
This first book in the new JENNIE MCGRADY MYSTERY SERIES promises intrigue and adventure for young adults. Jennie's summer seems perfect until her grandmother disappears with a million dollars in stolen diamonds. When Jennie enlists Ryan's help in finding Gram, a dangerous search looms ahead.

The Race by Lauraine Snelling
The captivating first book in the GOLDEN FILLY SERIES. Sixteen-year-old Tricia Evanston has loved horses as long as she can remember, and her father has been training her to compete professionally. But when her dad ends up in the hospital, it's up to Trish to win the big race.